THE FINAL RUSH

Book 2 in the Vitala Vipers Saga

A DreadBall Novel

by Robert E Waters

The Final Rush
By Robert E. Waters
Cover by Giorgio de Michele

Zmok Books an imprint of
Winged Hussar Publishing, LLC, 1525 Hulse Road, Unit 1, Point Pleasant, NJ 08742

PB 978-1-950423-89-7
EB 978-1-958872-60-4

Library of Congress No. 2024939555

Bibliographical references and index
1. Science Fiction 2. Games 3. Action & Adventure

For more information on Winged Hussar Publishing, LLC, visit us at:
https://WHPsupplyroom.com
https://www.WingedHussarPublishing.com

Twitter: WingHusPubLLC
Facebook: Winged Hussar Publishing LLC

THE FINAL RUSH

Welcome to the Warpath universe!

Humanity rules the galaxy through an organization known as the Galactic Co-Prosperity Sphere (GCPS). Thousands of suns and hundreds of thousands of planets revolve around this economic and technological juggernaut. Life is good.

But within this comfortable co-prosperity lies a relentless drive for self-governance. Alien races, for centuries having suffered under the corporate yolk, rebel against the GCPS and take what is theirs. War is constant. No one is truly safe... or prosperous.

Thus comes DreadBall, the deadliest sports event in the universe.

Teams from all over the GCPS commit their best and brightest players in a do-or-die struggle for fame, glory, and wealth. Heroes and legends rise and fall in the DreadBall arena while their corporate sponsors line their pockets with unimaginable wealth. DreadBall is a test of wills that only the bravest, only the strongest, survive.

The 'strikers' are the ball-carriers, the scorers, the most nimble, most agile of the DreadBall elite. They lack the power of the guards, but their abilities in the arena are the subject of the most awe-inspiring legends in the GCPS. If you need a score, strikers are your best option.

The 'guards' are the muscle, the true hammers of the DreadBall arena. They are not equipped to carry the ball, but they wouldn't want to anyway. Their hands are for slamming, choking, injuring, and if the DreadBall Governing Body (DGB, or 'Digby' for short) continues to allow it, for killing. Entire teams have been wiped out by a guard on rampage.

The 'jacks' serve the DreadBall arena in a wide variety of ways.

They are, in essence, a combination of the other two specialist roles.

Reasonably agile and fast, they can score, though their ball-carrying skills are not as refined as those of the striker. They often serve as field captains and assistant coaches, and they have a talent for blocking opponents from scoring lanes.

And finally, the DreadBall glove. Every striker and jack wears a special glove in order to catch, carry, and throw the ball which can oftentimes move at speeds of up to 200 miles per hour. Every race and team has a specially-designed glove to fit their physiology and play style. Without this glove, a lot of hands would be ripped away. DreadBall is a bloody sport, indeed, but let's not get carried away!

So, now you know some basics of the game. The teams are assembled, the ball is ready for release. Grab a snack, a drink, find a comfortable seat in the stands, and get ready to cheer.

DreadBall begins... now!

Prologue

987AE, Kaala Pani Prison, Third Sphere Industrial World Vitala, Zaigor System

Saanvi Kapoor stared in abject rage at the vid screen in front of her. She could not believe the words being spoken by that back-stabbing coach and her useless brother.

"Leeland Roth! Leeland Roth! How does it feel to be going back home?"

"Well… if you mean going back to the Sphere in which I played DreadBall as a member of the Trontek 29ers, then it feels pretty good. My home, as it were, is in the Second Sphere. I haven't been back there since I was a child and don't intend on going back any time soon."

"You will be playing against the 29ers at least once, possibly twice, during the season. Any concerns or apprehensions about that?"

"No more than for any other team we might play against. The 29ers are a solid team, no matter their players, their coaching staff. Perennial favorites. They'll be tough, but we're ready to face any and all challenges."

"Any final comment about putting the Vitala Vipers into top league play?"

"No, not at all. We've got good players, good coaches. We're ready."

"Aryan Kapoor! Your sister Saanvi is currently serving a twenty-five year prison sentence, without parole, for conspiracy and sedition. How do you feel about that?"

"Well, I probably feel the same way most brothers might feel about it. I'm not happy with it. I wish things had turned out differently for her. But there is hope that she will come out a better person, realizing that what she did was a terrible crime against me, the family, the corporation, and herself. I hope she finds Vishnu."

"Will you be travelling with the team to the First Sphere?"

"Oh, yes. Eventually. I have to. I hear the First Sphere throws the best parties."

Laughter...

Saanvi jumped from her chair, screamed, and tried kicking the vid screen. A guard stopped her.

"Now, now, Saanvi," he said, picking her up in a bear hug and setting her back down. "You've already destroyed two screens this month. One more, and they'll put you back in isolation. For a whole month this time."

"Unhand me, you Zwerm!" she cried, trying to break free from his powerful grasp, strands of her pitch-black hair covering her face. "Let me destroy that blasted screen or turn it off. I've had enough!"

An inmate sitting nearby, who knew better than to challenge Ms. Kapoor, muted the interview. Saanvi struggled a little longer, then calmed. "If I have to hear my brother's voice one more time, I'll..."

What could she do? Like the media said, she was serving a twenty-five year sentence, with no chance of parole, for sedition and for conspiring with Rebs to attack and capture a GCPS cruiser. And all of this on the word, the confession, of a Gaelian jack who did not understand the meaning of 'discretion.' *I should have known better*, she thought as she settled, under duress, back into her chair, beads of sweat covering her dark forehead. The silence of the inmate common room was refreshing.

Leeland was right on one score, she thought. *A Reb is*

only as loyal as the flow of his money, the imperatives of his agenda, and the threat to his life. The Gaelian had squawked on that last item.

I should have known better...

But she didn't need her useless brother lecturing her about finding Vishnu, finding peace. Where did he get off prancing in front of the media like the good child, acting all mature and suave to their store-bought accolades? Didn't they remember that he was a self-centered drunk who spent their father's money wallowing in his own vomit in any gutter he found most comfortable? He was the one who had conspired with Rebs. Couldn't they see it? Or did they choose not to because he and his sniveling little DreadBall team were now the darlings of the sports world? The Vitala Vipers were heading to league competition in the FSIDL, the First Sphere Intergalactic DreadBall League. Naturally, the media had elected to hype the good parts of that reality, ignoring the bad. But if there was some way that she could shed light on the bad parts, well...

How could she? There was no escaping Kaala Pani prison. Its security measures were unparalleled.

Saanvi had tested the system on her third day. In her baggy, oversized purple jumpsuit, she had walked straight through the lobby, across the exercise yard, and toward the main gate. She was ordered three times to stop; she refused. At ten meters from the gate, she was struck by a bolt of energy arcing out from the guard tower. A week later, she woke up in the infirmary with a nasty headache and a three-inch second-degree burn on her back. Rest and a successful skin graft had put her body back in order, but she never tried that again. Her family name and its corporation were influential, yes, but even they couldn't spring her from Kaala Pani. Not for the crime she had *allegedly* committed.

So, how? How could she show the media the truth, about her brother, about the team, about Leel—

"I'd like to make my monthly vid call now, Barnard," she said to the guard who had saved her from another session of isolation.

"You've already made your call this month, Saanvi," he said. "You cannot make another."

Saanvi stood, adjusted her jumpsuit, and said with a smile, "Let me make this call, Barnard, and I'll take good care of your family."

She still had contacts within Kapoor Industries, and during her call sessions, she had set up ghost accounts for three of the guards serving Kaala Pani. Like her corporation, they did not have the clout to help her escape (that could mean execution for all three), but for the right price, a guard could look the other way, bend the rules just a little, feign ignorance when questioned.

Barnard seemed to struggle with the offer. He looked left, right, ensuring that no one of import was near enough to hear. Then he said, quietly, "Okay, Saanvi, just this once. But it better be a sizable gift this time. Last time wasn't much."

"Hey, the gift is commiserate with the favor," she said, following the big oaf to the communications room. "Trust me, Barnard. This is a *big* favor. And I'll need some privacy. No spies riding the stream this time."

"Now you know I can't promise that, Saanvi," he said, passing his card over the maglock and opening the comm room door. The lights came on immediately. "None of us can."

"Yes, but you can still talk to the guy," she said, flashing a big, bright smile, "and see if he'll take his break, can't you?"

Barnard sighed, let her in, and directed her to a vid screen in the back of the room. "I'll do what I can. But I ain't making no promises, girl."

Saanvi nodded and took her seat.

Each prisoner was allowed one call per month, and sometimes two if there was a crisis in their family or within their corporation. At Kaala Pani, the inmates were not entirely cut off from the world, nor from their business if they still had connections therein. But the calls were heavily monitored. A comm guard, behind a two-way mirror, listened in and could cut the call if he or she deemed the conversation problematic, and every word was transcribed for later review. Nothing she said to any outside source could be totally private. But sometimes...

She placed her long fingers on the comm board, and it flicked to life. Within seconds, her head was swimming in a sea of virtual images, touch panels, eye and facial recognition sensors, and voice monitor buoys. The buoys appeared only for a second, then flicked away. Saanvi smiled. *Good job, Barnard. You get another five thousand and a big, wet kiss.*

"*State the number you are calling, Saanvi Kapoor, Serial Number 32576,*" a light female voice cooed through the virtual clutter. "*Number and purpose for call.*"

She stated the number and ended with what she always said. "Small talk."

But not today. Today, the conversation would be important, serious, and would put into motion the end game that she had intended to reach with that attack on the GCPS cruiser, the *Dread*. Her mistake had been relying on Rebs to carry her message. This time, she would use a source closer to home.

A member of the family.

A light *ping!* indicated a successful connection with her number, and a soft, unassuming pixelated face appeared. The face smiled, nodded, and said, "*What can I do for you today, Ms. Kapoor?"*

Saanvi paused, collected her clever thoughts, and said with a pep that belied the frustration festering just below her skin. "Mr. D, I need you to contact Manan. I have a little job for him."

Chapter 1

Third Sphere Industrial World Vitala, Zaigor System, Kapoor Industries Complex

Leeland Roth placed his hand on the digital scanner. A flash of bright red light acknowledged the placement, scanned his palm quickly, and confirmed success with a happy *beep!*

Acceptance of his new contract was now signed, certified, and completed. He breathed a sigh of relief but missed his old Xtreme DreadBall days when a handshake and a signature from a common pen were enough to seal the deal. Doing it this way almost felt like he was selling his soul. And perhaps he was. A three-year extension of his service as head coach for the Vitala Vipers was a sweet deal, especially with all the financial incentives he was agreeing to. But everything had to go just right for him to receive those incentives, and that's where his joy ended. Nothing in life (and *his* life, particularly) ever played out according to plan.

"Don't look so glum, Coach," Aryan Kapoor said, leaning back in his plush office chair and curling his fingers together behind a head of thick black hair. His brown eyes sparkled. "You just signed a contract that will make you one of the richest coaches in the sport. It is a day of celebration."

Leeland nodded and pushed the scanner tablet across the table toward his boss. "My happy dance can wait, Aryan. In less than two hours, we'll be sliding out of the Zaigor System en route to Hope and to our first season in the FSIDL. There are scores of things to finalize and not enough time to do so. And now you tell me that you won't be coming with us. What's that all about?"

Aryan sighed deeply, removed his hands from behind his head, and crossed them over his chest. "Since Saanvi is no longer head of the family, I have... obligations that I must attend to. I'm not head of Kapoor Industries, true, but still head of the family. It's nothing more than a ceremonial position, I grant you, but nevertheless, I must attend to the family's public persona. Weddings and conferences to attend, contracts to sign, ribbons to cut, babies to kiss. The Kapoor family is rather large, Leeland: aunts, uncles, cousins." Aryan chuckled. "Larger than I remember. But then, I wasn't really thinking of anything serious while I was drowning in booze in those gutters. I will follow you to Hope. I promise. It's just a delay, nothing more."

In truth, Leeland was more proud than angry with what Aryan was saying. When they had first met, Aryan was just a spoiled little rich kid who had recently crawled out of one of those gutters. At the time, Leeland wasn't far from that reality either. They had both matured since that fateful day in that cold, smelly Xtreme locker room. But Aryan's maturity had surprised Leeland. The boy was growing up fast, and that was a great thing to see. The concern he had was Aryan's sister.

Saanvi would be spending the next twenty-five years in Kaala Pani for her seditious crimes. But what protections did the boy have to thwart any attempts that she might make to exploit and manipulate him from behind those thick walls? Since her incarceration, Leeland had made a point to keep tabs on her and to keep Aryan away from bad influences. So far, Saanvi had been quiet, though he had learned that she, on occasion, spent a megacredit or two to make a call. No nefarious activity yet on those calls, but would that last, and could Leeland keep Aryan safe from her tentacles once they were separated by hundreds upon hundreds upon thousands of light years?

The answer was a resounding no.

"Very well," Leeland said, rubbing his fingers through his newly trimmed hair—a little grayer nowadays than he preferred, "but follow as soon as you can. Our success in league play will be directly proportionate to the stability of the coaching staff and the Viper front office. You're the front office, Aryan. We need you."

That last compliment put the pep in Aryan's demeanor. He stood, smiled broadly, and offered his hand. "Thank you, Leeland. I and the Kapoor family appreciate all that you have done for the Vipers. You have put our humble little planet of Vitala on the stellar map." He winked. "Now, get the hell out of my office and earn your new contract. The First Sphere—and *glory*—awaits."

Leeland smiled and took the boy's hand. He agreed with the first thing Aryan had said, but not so much the second.

***

"Don't make me beg, Carla," Leeland said, finalizing the Vipers' uniform and equipment supply list. He tapped his acceptance on the tablet and handed it over to one of the shuttle pilots. "Sign the three-year deal."

Carla 'Bullseye' Bock shook her head and handed her own tablet to the shuttle pilot. "I've already signed the one-year extension, Leelee. That's sufficient for now."

"I need you for three."

"You get one."

"The Banshees have signed Sheera Rainwaters to a

four-year deal," he said, turning to his defensive coach and longtime friend. "They aren't going to be calling on you any time soon. The I-Corps Tigers have disbanded. Your head coaching options at the moment are basically nil. Three years is nothing, Carla. *Give* me three years."

She shook her head. "You get one."

Grrrr! He wanted to scream his frustration right in her face. *This woman!* She drove him crazy sometimes. Her refusal to sign Aryan's three-year offer was so infuriating... and yet, at this point in the Vitala Vipers' history, getting Bullseye Bock back for one year was a gift. *I should be thankful*, he thought. And he was thankful. After what had happened during the tournament, how Bullseye had decided to leave the team after 'Backhoe' Bertuchi's mortal sacrifice, having her agree to come back at all was a stroke of great fortune and luck. Leeland would take the year, indeed, but he wasn't about to let her go after that one year without a fight.

The same was true for Conner Newberg. After harsh injuries suffered during the tournament championship game, he had decided to retire as a player and devote himself to being the Vipers' jack coach and personnel manager/ recruiter. He too had signed only a one-year extension and was just as intransigent as Bullseye in his blatant refusal to sign Aryan's longer deal. His and Bullseye's decisions were incredibly selfish. That, too, Leeland understood well.

Both of them were now eyeing head coaching gigs of their own. A one-year deal for the Vipers in a First Sphere league was just the audition they needed to catch the greedy eye of some First or Second Sphere corporate team. DreadBall, Leeland had realized long ago, was not only brutal on the pitch, but off of it as well.

Conner Newberg emerged from the team shuttle, the second in a line of four waiting to depart.

"Well," he said, blowing a strand of messy hair out of his eyes, "everything is set."

"All team members on the shuttle?" Leeland asked.

Conner nodded. "Yes. That's including Jimbo, who continues to complain that he's riding coach. He's still sore at you for refusing to allow him to take his Chevron 80 with him."

Leeland shrugged. "With the money he's being paid, he can buy a new car when we get to Hope. A better one, actually."

"And you tell him that if he doesn't like his seat," Bullseye said with a wry smile, "we can find him a new one on the shuttle wing."

"The press is going to be on that slide cruiser," Leeland said, putting his signature on one last tablet and handing it over to the shuttle crew lead. Everything was now in place and ready to go. "They'll be looking for any excuse to accentuate the negative. The Vipers need to show a unified front. We all arrive together, enthusiastic and determined in our mission, ready to play. We give them no room to go negative."

Conner curled his mouth and nodded approval. "Impressive, Boss. I'm glad to see you finally realizing the value of media manipulation."

"Actually, that was my idea," Bullseye said, grabbing her carry-on and heading up the ramp of shuttle one. "Coach Roth still finds the whole concept... tedious."

"My job is to coach the team," Leeland said, following Bullseye up the ramp, "not cater to gossip columnists."

Conner laughed and followed. "That's why you got us, eh, Coach Roth?"

"If you guys keep calling me by my last name, I'll—"

"Oh, just strap yourself in and pipe down," Bullseye barked, giving Leeland a light shove. "Time to go."

Leeland took the first seat in the shuttle and strapped in tightly. He was never good at dealing with the strong Gs pulled escaping the atmosphere of any planet, not just Vitala. Once on the cruiser, he'd be fine. He just hoped he didn't lose his lunch before he got there.

"Oh, one more thing," he said, pulling on his straps to lean forward and catch Conner's eye. "How we doing on recruitment?"

Conner nodded. "We'll be fine. I've scheduled three days of tryouts once we reach the new facility. Jacks and guards are our greatest need right now, though we do need another striker as well. We'll flesh out the team before the first game. I promise. And I think you'll like some of the names I've invited to camp."

Leeland almost always approved of Conner's choices. The guy had a keen eye for talent, especially for jacks and strikers. Not so much for guards, but Bullseye would help fill in the gaps for that position. As the Vipers' defensive coach and as an ex-corporate Marine sniper, she had a keen eye for violence; and that was the name of the game for DreadBall guards.

They still had positions to fill on the team, and Conner was on top of it. Leeland was glad of that. More importantly, he was glad that so many of their tournament players had agreed to extend their contracts. Little Frankie (whose serious injury against the Saltborne Sledgehammers had put his career in question) and Jimbo Threpe (his injury had been equally concerning); both had recovered. Spencer Mills. Shadrack Menapi. Jerold Minata. The starting lineup had yet to be solidified; it would be impractical to establish that when so many slots on the team still needed filling. But it was always easier to coach players that you knew and whose talents and skills you respected, even if they were divas like

Jimbo Threpe.

The shuttle ramp closed, the cabin compressed. It was time to go.

Leeland braced himself, gripping the armrests of his chair with white knuckles. He was excited and scared. There, he admitted to himself. He was scared. He shouldn't be. He had been in this DreadBall business as player and now as head coach most of his life. He had seen everything; nothing about the game surprised him anymore. And yet, moving from the Third Sphere to the First was like—he shook his head and couldn't forgive himself for the pun—a whole new ball game. Same game, same rules. But the competition was at a level that most of the Viper players had never experienced before. In the Third Sphere tournament, they had played against teams with scrub players mostly, found in the deepest recesses of back-alley worlds and gutter planets. In the end, some of those teams proved quite skillful. Some exceeded expectations.

First Sphere teams and players, however, represented a whole other level of competition. First Sphere teams, like the Trontek 29ers, were in it for keeps, and could the Vipers stand against them? If not, 'Coach Roth' could be presiding over a graveyard by game three.

The shuttle lifted and began its ascent to the slide cruiser that lay in low orbit above planet Vitala. Leeland braced for thrust.

Bullseye put her hand on his arm and stared at him with her brilliant velvet eyes. She whispered. "Leelee, I know you are disappointed with me and Conner for not giving you a three-year commitment. But I promise you, on my honor, I will not abandon you this time. You have me for the whole season. I promise."

Leeland smiled at his defensive coach. She still

possessed the same black hair streaked with grey that she had on their first meeting. And she was still as big and as formidable as ever. Leeland nodded and loosened his grip on the armrests. He relaxed into his chair and thought, *If you're telling me the truth, Carla, then we'll be able to deal with any hazards along the way.*

The shuttle ignited its engines.

If you're telling me the truth...

Chapter 2

Carooda Mansion, First Sphere, Mu'Shen'Wan Temple

Le Zuan Carooda and his young partner faced each other on a hover plank that dipped slightly with their collective weight. The plank itself was only eight feet long, two feet wide; an incorrect move, a slip of the foot, a lapse of discipline could easily cast one or both of them off the plank. His partner was young, inexperienced, but dedicated to the forms of the Mu'Shen'Wan. The question before Le Zuan was: *is he dedicated enough?*

He raised his left leg and leaped forward two feet, letting the soft hoof of his right foot hit the board on its edge and dip the plank even further. The novitiate across from him compensated and leaped just when Le Zuan's hoof came down, thus avoiding the concussive shift of the plank and coming back down in good balance on both legs.

"Very good, Remome," Le Zuan said, his lithe grey Judwan arms and hands making the appropriate forms in response. "You anticipated my move and compensated accordingly. Are you maintaining deep meditation?"

The young Judwan nodded, his eyes closed. "Yes, Master Carooda. Your image is clear in dream-state."

Not for long, Le Zuan thought but did not say aloud. Now would come the move, the form, that rarely failed to toss them.

He backed away from Remome, closed his own eyes, and remembered his days as a striker for the Pelgar Mystics. What wonderful days those were, when he'd been young, vibrant, and determined, just like the young Judwan on the wobbling plank before him.

Le Zuan bent at his knees, felt his aged bones pop quietly, reached through his mind into dream-state, and pulled a weapons-grade titanium ball from the haze of memory. Unlike most of the other races that played the game, Judwans did not require electromagnetic gloves to catch the ball, nor did they require one to throw it. Their long arms and fingers were well-suited to fire the ball across the pitch at speeds equaling or exceeding anything those cumbersome gloves could produce.

Le Zuan followed the forms of the Mu'Shen'Wan perfectly, thrusting his arms out toward his novitiate, reaching out with well-manicured talons, making sure the boy confused the moment with standard practice.

Then he pulled his arm back in dream-state and launched the ball at Remome's chest.

To the novitiate, it appeared in his trance like a real ball, and he responded exactly as Le Zuan expected.

First, Remome panicked and balked. A second later, he tried twitching to the right to avoid being struck, but he over-twitched and then made the further mistake of allowing inertia to carry him over the side. He tried reaching out to catch the plank with his flailing arms, but he missed and fell ten feet to the hardwood floor of the temple.

Remome hit the floor and screamed.

Le Zuan came out of his trance and lowered the plank to the floor. "No shouting in my temple," he said, letting the plank settle comfortably and turning off its anti-grav pulsars. "Maintain your discipline."

Remome gripped his broken shoulder. "Yes, Master Carooda. I apologize for my weakness. I have failed you. I will—"

Le Zuan put up his hand for silence. "Steady now, my

boy. You are my best student this semester. I tricked you. I pulled something from my own memories and forced it into your dream-state. You failed to recognize it as an illusion, got confused, and reacted inappropriately. You aren't the first to fall for it. But you will learn from this mistake and return better prepared to know the difference between what is real and what is fake."

A human-like medibot slipped into the room and grabbed the collar of the novitiate's robe. "Study your forms," Le Zuan said before the boy was tugged away. "Your shoulder will be repaired posthaste. Then, eat, study, and return to me as the sun sets. We will try again."

"Yes, Master Carooda."

Remome was pulled away, and Le Zuan turned toward a strong pillar of white light being cast across his temple floor from a setting sun. The day was well into the afternoon; a perfect time for personal meditation.

Le Zuan adjusted his red robe, retightened the white belt at his waist, and sat on his prayer mat in lotus form. He closed his eyes against the warm, inviting ray of light. He breathed deeply, held it for several seconds, then exhaled. He was ready.

A knock came at his door.

He sighed, opened his eyes, and said, "Yes, what is it?"

His personal bodyguard, Roiu, poked in his slender head. "Forgive me, Le Zuan. But there is a human begging admittance."

"A human? What is its name?"

"Manan Kapoor."

Le Zuan raised his brow.

***

The tea Le Zuan poured into Manan Kapoor's cup was a blend of dried flowers and stems of artichoke, chamomile, jasmine, and lotus flower. Its aroma was intoxicating, and Le Zuan breathed in its fragrant steam. His human visitor seemed less impressed, though he was at least respectful enough to keep his opinions to himself.

"It's a family recipe," Le Zuan said, pouring a cup of his own. "Designed to calm the nerves, soothe the senses. Judging from your agitated state and less-than-immaculate attire, Mr. Kapoor, you appear to need it. I assume you travelled far to reach me?"

Manan carefully picked up his cup of hot tea and took a sip. He took another and set the cup down, cleared his throat. "Yes, all the way from the Zaigor System, Third Sphere."

Le Zuan finished pouring his own tea and sat down across the table from his visitor. "Yes, I'm familiar with that system. And too, Kapoor Industries. But I don't recall a member of your family ever travelling all the way to the First Sphere. To what do I owe the honor?"

Manan took another sip of his tea, apparently growing fond of its scent and taste. That, and perhaps the light sedative that Roiu dropped in to ensure the human's proper behavior. A sedative that worked on human beings, not Judwan. "I'll come right to the point. My uncle, Damon Kapoor, recently died, leaving the company to his children."

"My condolences."

Manan nodded. "He was a cold, bitter man whom I did not care for. The universe is better without him. However, his daughter Saanvi is now in prison for conspiring with Rebs to attack a GCPS cruiser which nearly killed two entire DreadBall teams during tournament play. Her brother, a sniveling little cretin known as Aryan, opted to turn over the company to the board, but now he is en route to—you have absolutely no idea what I'm talking about, do you, Master Carooda?"

Le Zuan took another sip and said, "My duties and obligations are many, Mr. Kapoor, and the stars are legion. I cannot stay abreast of everything that occurs amidst the thousands upon thousands of habitable planets between here and Vitala."

"But you are a gangster, am I correct? You do run a vast criminal enterprise that reaches into the Third Sphere, isn't that so?"

In human parlance, yes indeed: Le Zuan Carooda was a gangster. He liked to refer to himself as a 'businessman,' fulfilling a need that the GCPS could not fulfill for its many non-human communities living within its vast reaches. But 'gangster' would suffice.

There was no communication network into or out of his temple. No spooks listening in. Le Zuan felt comfortable speaking the truth aloud. "Indeed I am, Mr. Kapoor. And how perfect a visage: an ex-DreadBall player, a Judwan pacifist, teaching Mu'Shen'Wan to any and all who seek inner peace."

"So your teachings and this temple are a ruse, a front?" Manan asked.

"Oh, no, my good fellow. The temple and the teachings are real and as important to me as drawing breath. They are merely the public face of my true purpose in life."

"And that is...?"

Le Zuan smiled. "Robbing the GCPS blind." Le Zuan set down his tea. "Now, forgive me if I am too blunt, but stop playing games with me, Mr. Kapoor. State your purpose for being here or finish your tea and see yourself out."

Manan took a final sip of his tea, cleared his throat, and got to the point. "Aryan Kapoor's DreadBall team, the Vitala Vipers, recently won a tournament which has allowed them to join the FSIDL. You are familiar with that league, I assume?"

"Of course."

"Good. The team is currently en route to Hope, where they will take possession of their new training facility." He seemed to pause for effect. Le Zuan was about to call in Roiu and have him escort this useless human out. Then Manan Kapoor said a name that Le Zuan thought he'd never hear again.

"Leeland Roth is the head coach of the Vitala Vipers."

A long pause levitated between them. It was then Manan's turn to sound smug. "You certainly know that name, don't you, Le Zuan Carooda? A name I'm sure you'll never forget. Now... do I have *your* undivided attention, or are you going to keep flexing on me?"

The Roth brothers were the proverbial thorn in Le Zuan's side. How could he forget them?

He had the misfortune of playing both the Trontek 29ers and the Jade Dragons in quick succession during his last season, seven years past. A mid-season slam from a Greenmoon Smackers guard had hobbled him somewhat as he entered both games. First up was Leeland Roth, who used moves against Le Zuan such that he looked like a rank amateur. The arrogant human striker had stolen the ball from his powerful grip at least three times during regulation. Then came Victor Roth, sealing Le Zuan's fate and humiliation by using moves that left him wallowing on the pitch in his own bitter tears. A Dragon guard then came up and took him out of commission. Le Zuan had recovered from the devastating slam, but the media was relentless in their declaration that the great Le Zuan Carooda was done, finished, *kaput!* All the rumors about his demise, and even all the jokes and disrespect from his own teammates and coach, eventually forced his retirement.

Yes, he hated the Roth brothers. Loathed them with as much hatred as any Judwan could muster.

But Le Zuan did not subscribe to the old adage that the past was prologue. No. The past *was* the past, and now, seven years later, it seemed petty to rekindle old hatreds and resentments. No. He needed to move forward with the life he had now and forget about the past. These days, he could buy and sell the Roth brothers ten times over.

He brushed off the name by waving his long gray fingers through the air as if he were shooing a fly. "What is that name to me now? I care not."

"Maybe this will make you care."

Manan pulled a pen from his vest pocket and a small strip of paper. He scribbled a number on the paper and slid it over to Le Zuan.

Le Zuan pinched the paper strip between two of his three fingers and read it many times. "Megacredits?"

"Indeed."

"And what, pray tell, do you wish me to do for such a generous payment?"

"A simple task, really. Through your ample network, Saanvi and I would like you to find and reveal Victor Roth's sordid background. The truth of it is there, Master Carooda. You know it as well as I. Leeland Roth's youngest brother was no saint, no angel. Leeland was responsible for his death, true, and perhaps it was an accident as he has claimed." Manan leaned over the table and winked. "And perhaps it was no accident at all. Perhaps Victor's transgressions—and they were legion as you say, by all accounts—had gotten too toxic for even his older brother to endure. A burst of planned violence on the DreadBall pitch, and problem solved. The truth—all of it—is there. You simply need to find it and let it rise to the surface like gas bubbles from a swamp. Let the bubbles grow and burst and spread their vile scent everywhere."

Le Zuan was beginning to like this simian humanoid. Not only did he use low tech to convey monetary incentives (what's a single number on a piece of paper to a nosey investigator, but an untraceable chain of numerals?), but he had an eloquence many humans lacked.

"And if you do this thing I ask of you and the end result is Leeland Roth's demise," Manan continued, "that number will double. Triple if you do something else as well."

Triple the value would go a long, long way to help Le Zuan and his people reclaim their home planet of Pelgar, which had been ruthlessly overtaken by the GCPS, and to this day, was still being stripped of its vast mineral wealth. Yes, three times the number would go far in righting that great wrong.

"What is this other thing, Mr. Kapoor?" Le Zuan asked. "Quickly, now. My time is precious."

Manan cleared his throat again. "We want Jimbo Threpe, aka 'Mackinaw' Jim, killed. He's the Vitala Vipers' lead striker."

"Hmm. I see. And why, sir?"

Manan shook his head. "It is best I do not say, other than Saanvi doesn't like him. That's reason enough."

No, it wasn't, but Le Zuan did not bother pressing the matter. "Mr. Kapoor, you must know that assassination is not in the—shall we say—Judwan DNA. The mere thought of killing someone goes against everything we stand for, despite our brutal past with the GCPS. I am a gangster, yes, and violence is sometimes a means to an ends, but murder? No, sir. That will not be thought on, nor will I entertain the possibility. No amount of money will make me abandon the imperatives of my culture.

"However, I will accept your first request. The chance to double this number is well worth the effort and risk. But no murder, and we will not speak of it again. Agreed?"

Le Zuan sat there and watched as Manan ground his teeth as if he were chewing stones. He found it surprising that the human did not seem passive or subdued by the sedative placed in his tea. *Perhaps his constitution is iron,* he thought, *or perhaps he had taken an antidote prior to his arrival.* If the latter, Manan Kapoor was even cleverer than he thought. *And someone to watch very carefully.*

"Very well," Manan said, inflating somewhat in Le Zuan's piercing glare. "You accept my first request?"

Le Zuan nodded. "Yes."

"Then we have a deal. And a verbal one only. I never sign my name or agree virtually or in any other manner to anything. My word is my bond; I think you can appreciate that. That number before you will be transferred to the account of your choosing within thirty-two hours; a goodwill gesture from Saanvi to you. Even if you fail in this endeavor, it is yours. No harm, no foul. Once the deed is accomplished, an equal amount will be transferred again. Now, if you will excuse me, Master Carooda, I will trouble you no longer." Manan rose from the table. "I must go and find an assassin."

Le Zuan escorted Manan to the door. When they reached it, a thought came to mind. "This is your lucky day, Mr. Kapoor. I will not do the killing for you, but I know someone who can. And he's good. Very, very good."

"Who?" Manan asked.

"Go to Gaylor, third planet of the Gosch System," Le Zuan said, "and find a creature called The Whip."

"The Whip?"

Le Zuan nodded and smiled as he began to fall again into trance. "Yes... The Whip."

Chapter 3

Planet Hope, First Sphere

Hello to DreadBall fans everywhere! I'm Elmer...

And I'm Dobbs...

And we're here today to witness the arrival of the Vitala Vipers. Look at that crowd gathered around the team's shuttle, Dobbs. I'd call it a mob, wouldn't you?

Indeed I would, Elmer, and twice on Sunday. Stands to reason, for this most unlikely team battled through personal (and personnel) losses, injuries, death, scandal, and came out smelling like a Tanjur Rose at the end of the most exciting and brutal tournament in recent years to determine which Third Sphere team would have the honor of playing in the big leagues, the First Sphere Intergalactic DreadBall League, or to you uninitiated out there, the FSIDL.

Don't insult our viewers, Dobbs. Our ratings are low enough. Who would have thought that an old, washed up, nearly forgotten ex-Trontek 29er could cobble together such a rag-tag bunch of misfits and perimeter riffraff and make them the darlings of the upcoming FSIDL season? Well, that coach, Leeland Roth, sure thought he could.

And here he comes now, Elmer, followed by Carla 'Bullseye' Bock, one of the toughest ladies I know in all the universe, and Conner Newberg, who has set aside the uniform for a cushy coaching job.

Oh, I would never call a coaching job on a DreadBall team cushy, Dobbs. Not unless I wanted to get punched in the face.

Which you do quite often, Elmer, much to my

amusement. Now here comes the team...

First for the Vipers we have Franklin 'Little Frankie' Marbary, a striker who almost met his god in the tournament championship game against the Saltborne Sledgehammers. But he looks no worse for wear now, and definitely one to watch. Next up, Spencer Mills, another Viper striker who showed some real promise in the tournament. One wonders, though, if the higher level of competition in the First Sphere will be too much for him.

And here comes Shadrack Menapi, clearly the Vipers' top guard these days, especially after the devastating loss of Brutus 'Triple-B' Backhoe Bertuchi, may he rest in pieces.

Too soon, Dobbs, too soon. Allow me to take over this roster review before they cut us off the air for your cheeky monologue.

There's Caesar 'Maddog' King, a new guard recently signed by the Vipers. I don't know a lot about him, other than that he too once played on a convict team like the former Triple-B. He's less enigmatic than Triple-B used to be, as I understand it, which belies his nickname, but we'll see how it goes. DreadBall has a way of taming even the most vicious dog.

And here come the jacks: Jerold Minata, Lucas Buck, and Artemis Hale. We've seen Minata in action: a solid player that Conner Newberg cannot say enough good things about. Buck and Hale are recent additions, but are young, vibrant, and ready to prove themselves. But overconfident, cocky boys like them often prove themselves right into an early grave.

And finally, saving the best for last, here comes Jimbo 'Mackinaw' Threpe. Oh, what a splendid creature he is. Look at all that bling, Dobbs. He's putting a major hurt on my vision. I can't decide whether to look away or ask for his hand in marriage.

He must have back trouble toting around all that gold, Elmer. But let's look beyond the flash. There is no doubting Jimbo's skills. He's one of the best passers in the game today, so he's literally worth *his weight in gold.*

So there you have it, gentles all. The Vitala Vipers.

Yeah, but they've got a lot of slots to fill, Dobbs. Too many, in my mind, to be ready by opening game.

Normally, I'd agree with you, Elmer. But this is Leeland Roth's team, and if there's one thing the Third Sphere tournament taught us, it's to never count Leeland, and the Vitala Vipers, out.

I'll drink to that, Dobbs.

Me too, Elmer. The first rounds on you.

***

Leeland pushed his way through the mob of media, well-wishers, nay-sayers, and young girls cheering and dreaming for Jimbo Threpe. As far as he could tell, not a single other player on the team had even one sycophant in the crowd. He supposed that was for the best. So few knew anything about the Vitala Vipers, other than what they had seen through the narrow lens of the media. But soon, very soon, everyone would know of his team and players. They had come to Hope to compete in the upcoming FSIDL season, and by the gods of old Earth mythology, they would do just that.

A slender male figure pushed his way through the crowd and met Leeland at the halfway point—an Asterian, Leeland recognized, by the long, pointed ears. He offered his hand and shouted over the crowd. "Good afternoon, Coach Roth. I'm so grateful you and the Vipers have arrived. My name is Shapshir Goethe. I'll be your liaison to the FSIDL and to Digby during the season."

Leeland greeted the Asterian with a sharp nod. Then he pulled back his hand. "I wasn't informed of any team liaison."

Shapshir nodded. "Oh, yes, indeed. Every team in the FSIDL has a contact to the front office. And I'm so honored to be serving the Vipers in that capacity, Coach Roth. Please, follow me, and I'll get you and your team out of this mob."

Leeland turned and helped Bullseye shuffle the players along the narrow defile between packs of howling well-wishers. He had to pry two ladies off of Jimbo Threpe's back just to get him clear of the mob and into a stretch bus hovering just off the curb where the shuttle had dropped them off. Once everyone was comfortably in place on the bus, he ducked and climbed in himself, into the small forward cab where Bullseye, Conner, and Shapshir Goethe were waiting.

The mob descended on the hover bus. The driver pulled away carefully to ensure no one was injured. Once clear of bodies, he accelerated, and the bus ascended thirty meters and slipped into a stream of other vehicles making their way about Hope's vast and opulent capital city of Rosaria.

Conner made a whistling sound. "That was close. I didn't expect that kind of reception."

"The two Second Sphere teams that made the FSIDL this season did not meet with such fanfare," Shapshir said, reaching into a small, fully stocked refrigerator holding a champagne bottle. "The Vitala Vipers are the belle of the ball, as one might say. Everyone wants to know of Coach Roth and his unlikely band of misfit snakes."

"I'd hardly call us misfits," Bullseye said, accepting a glass filled with clear, sparkling champagne. "And don't ever refer to us as snakes, Shapshir, or you'll get on my bad side. The Vipers didn't make it here by luck, you know. They earned it. And it isn't like Leeland is unknown to the First Sphere. He was a Trontek 29er not that long ago."

"I agree ten-fold, Coach Bock, and my apologies for the ham-handed joke." Shapshir handed a glass of champagne to Conner. "Ah, but time slips away so quickly here in the hustle and bustle of the First Sphere. People aren't likely to remember what happened last week, let alone six years ago. It's like starting all over again for you, Coach Roth."

"None, thanks," Leeland said, waving off his glass. "Alcohol's an occupational hazard for me."

"Come on, Leelee," Bullseye said. "Have a sip, at least. I'll make sure you don't overindulge."

Leeland sighed, nodded, and accepted the glass. He raised it to his nose. Fresh, effervescent, wonderful. Exactly what he needed, and didn't need. "For you, Bullseye. But if I get drunk, you're to blame. We have work to do. We shouldn't be spending it pouring libations for something we haven't accomplished yet. We just stepped off a shuttle. That is all."

"This is just a toast to welcome you to Hope and to the FSIDL," Shapshir said. "And then I promise, Coach Roth, we will get right down to it."

They raised their glasses and clinked them in unison. Behind them, beyond a small two-way energy shield separating their cabin from the team compartment, the boys were pouring champagne as well, laughing, cheering, and insulting each other in many clever ways. In short, they were having a good time. *And so be it*, Leeland thought. *It's my job to be serious, contrary. It's theirs to enjoy their success.*

They finished their toast, and the hover bus turned to head into downtown Rosaria.

***

In the years Leeland had spent playing Xtreme DreadBall in Fourth Sphere exile, and as head coach for the Vipers, he had quite forgotten the opulence of a First Sphere city. Rosaria, for lack of a better word, popped with color. Its scores of high-rise towers, over one hundred meters each, stitched together with walkways, bristled with kinetic reds and greens and blues as the sun ricocheted from one glass wall to the next, giving the entire skyline a techno-colored glow as if a digital Impressionist or drip painter had swiped her broad brush over the landscape. Innumerable lines of hover cars sped through the tight spaces between buildings, accentuating the grid-like design of the city. Mundane wheeled vehicles took advantage of the wide streets that curled their way through the lower quadrants, completing the circulatory-like system that gave Rosaria the look and feel of a human body. Massive vid panels covered entire blocks, blaring their sales pitches, CorpsNet news feeds, and entertainment programming to the delight of the citizenry that hustled here and there on sidewalks continually cleaned by servo-bots scurrying under the heady weight of the human and alien masses living their lives.

From his safe and secure seat inside the hover bus, Leeland looked down on it all while listening to their new liaison, and Bullseye, chat.

"There will be no pre-season, I'm afraid," Shapshir said, "but you will have three weeks for practice and training before your opening game. That should also give you time to fill empty spots on the roster."

"Does that give us enough time to fill empty slots, Conner?" Bullseye asked.

He nodded. "It should. Tryouts start in a couple days, and to be honest, I already have my mind set on who I want that's still available in free agency. The tryouts are really a formality, more for the benefit of the public and media, unless for some reason these guys show up and tank their auditions."

"Which happens on occasion," Leeland said, interrupting, pulling himself away from the window. "Make sure we get a chance to see a wide swath of talent. I'd like to have a full roster with at least a week to spare, if not longer."

"Thy will be done, Boss," Conner said, nodding. "I'll take care of it."

Shapshir pushed a button, and a compartment between the chairs popped open. He pulled out a small sheet of paper and handed it to Bullseye. "Here's your schedule."

Bullseye took the sheet but held it between her thumb and index finger as if it were toxic. "How'd you get this? It isn't supposed to be made available to us for another two weeks."

Shapshir shrugged. "A lady in the Digby front office owed me a favor. I collected." He smiled and winked. "Read it now, read it carefully, and then give it back to me so that I can dispose of it."

Bullseye glanced at it quickly, handed it to Conner who did the same. When Leeland got it, he studied it more carefully.

"Of course," Leeland said with a big, agitated sigh. He rolled his eyes and shook his head. "We play Trontek first. Figures."

"The people want drama, Leelee," Bullseye said. "They crave it."

"Yeah, they want to drop me right into my personal nightmare. I've no desire to start this season against Trontek."

"Unfortunately," Shapshir said, "the schedule is set. No changing it now."

Leeland knew how the system worked. He hadn't

been out of First Sphere competition long enough to have forgotten how leagues and schedules functioned. But that didn't mean he had to like it.

Their first three games were against the Trontek 29ers, the Pelgar Mystics, and the Kushan Fangs. All away games. Game four would be their first home game against the Nemion Oceanics. Human, Judwan, Veer-myn, and Sphyr. In that order. *Terrific!*

"Sixteen regular season games," Leeland said, running down the list with his finger. "Looks like we play two games each against division rivals, and one game each against inner conference rivals."

"That's right," Shapshir said. "The FSIDL is not the only league in the First Sphere, mind you. There are many others. However, *ours* is divided into two conferences with two divisions each. Each division has six teams. Thus, twelve teams per conference. We're in the Core Conference, Sol and Hope Divisions. We're in the Hope Division."

Conner chuckled. "How appropriate."

"The other conference?" Bullseye asked.

"The Star Conference, Radner and Cascadia Divisions."

"So we only play inner conference games during the regular season?" Leeland asked to confirm. "None against the Star Conference?"

"Correct. The Vipers will not compete against any team in the Star Conference unless we make the midseason Ultimate match or the championship game."

The chances of that, in their first season, were slim to none, Leeland knew. On average, it took at least two seasons, if not more, for a new team to generate the skills and personnel to play in such games. There were exceptions, of course, and some of those exceptions were teams on their schedule, teams that had blasted onto the DreadBall circuit with explosive first season runs. "So, they're throwing in an Ultimate match, eh?"

"Yes," Shapshir said, punching numbers into their onboard guidance computer to give the hover bus driver final coordinates. "No all-star game for the FSIDL. An unfortunate truth of our sport, Coach Roth, is that many of the alien races that live and play within GCPS influence do not like playing side by side with human players, and vice-versa. Someday, perhaps that will change, but until then, the FSIDL has chosen an alternative plan, to not only entertain, but to give back to the community something more than just entertainment.

"The midseason break is an Ultimate match between the top team in each division. A four-team match, with major awards and trophies going to the winning team and players, and all profits going to charity."

"Nice," Conner said, nodding. "I like that."

Leeland did as well. "Yes, not a bad idea. Something for us to work toward: getting in that game. Eight games between now and then, I assume the 'top team' means the one with the most wins by the mid-point?"

"Precisely," Shapshir said. "Winning is the primary measure of success in the FSIDL."

As it was in all DreadBall leagues, Leeland knew. A midseason break with a charity game was a nice gesture, so long as the league front office was honest and transparent with the megacredits that it donated to its designated charity. It was one thing to declare generosity publicly; it was entirely another to actually see it through. Just how many middlemen would the proceeds go through before it reached the needy?

Leeland looked at the schedule once more. He committed the games to memory and then handed the paper back to Shapshir as requested.

The Asterian liaison crumbled the paper into a tiny ball

and popped it into his mouth. He chewed thrice and gulped it down.

"Wow!" Bullseye said, a look of surprise and mild humor crossing her face. "That's security."

"Unless they want to pump my stomach—or bowels—or target my second brain near my belly for the information," Shapshir said with a light, though sincere, humor and wink, "no one will ever find out."

The bus lowered quickly and worked itself into a lower tier of flowing traffic. Leeland turned his attention back to the window.

At this level, the city blocks were like alloy, carbon compound, and transparent monuments bunched together like canned Veer-myn meat. There were few gaps between buildings within each block, and the vid screens that dominated the sides of buildings were brighter and more defined at this level. On three of the screens, three different DreadBall matches were in progress. Leeland squinted to try to see if he could figure out the teams by their uniforms, but the bus moved too quickly for him to get a clear impression. Humans versus Marauders in one game, for sure; Nameless versus Zee in another. The third? The image was too fuzzy to know for certain, which meant either the connection was poor, or the game was being relayed through several communication buoys strewn throughout the First and Second Spheres. Leeland smiled. That was the advantage of playing in the First Sphere: Conner would have ample chances to watch a diverse number of matches for future recruitment opportunities.

The bus settled to ground level and came to a quiet stop in front of a mid-sized building of light red-and-gold-stained glass. "We're here," Shapshir said, waving his hand over the inside latch panel on the door. "Lady and gentlemen...

welcome to the Viper Arena and Training Complex."

Leeland stepped out of the bus. He stood beside Bullseye, his jaw open and nearly touching the sidewalk. "I—I didn't expect such an opulent facility, and one constructed so quickly."

"It's a converted GCPS bank," Shapshir said, staring up at the building in awe, "so the structure was there already. The domed arena behind it, however, is brand new and still under construction."

The complex spanned half the block and was at least twenty meters tall. A digital Viper logo flashed brilliantly left to right across its entire façade, and small pennant flags were positioned uniformly along its length. They snapped in the breeze flowing down the street. "All this for little old us, eh?" Leeland could hardly believe it.

"FSIDL wants this expansion to work, Coach Roth," Shapshir said. "If it does, then that gives incentive to expand again, and perhaps again. They want to become the *premiere* DreadBall league in the First Sphere, and so they want to ensure that the Vipers have the same level of support that every team in the league has. The same kind of facility, the same home arena, that every team has. The league has put a lot of money into this endeavor.

"That, and a hefty donation from Kapoor Industries."

The rest of the Vipers filed out of the bus and huddled around their coaches. Little Frankie sidled up to Leeland and stared up at the building with the same slack-jaw expression as his coach. The young striker's high-pitched whistle said it all. "Thank you, Aryan Kapoor."

Leeland couldn't argue with that.

Chapter 4

Planet Gaylor

A smooth weapons-grade titanium ball, no larger than a human man's head, was launched through a waterfall of toxic runoff from the dying city above. A bit of discarded human thigh bone that had washed down with the rest of the detritus from the radiated streets struck the ball and sent it spinning out of control at one hundred and fifty miles per hour. Right into the startled face of a Veer-myn striker.

The ball struck, and half the creature's head was torn away.

A Convict jack jumped over the ruined Veer-myn and scooped the loose ball off the slippery sewer floor and was gone.

Cegrich Wick snapped his whip.

"Die... all of you!" he shouted, baring his sharp, Veer-myn teeth and snapping his whip three more times. The dry, hollowed-out husk of his right eye socket ached.

The coach of the opposing Convict team gave a meaty chuckle at his side. "Another thousand you owe me, Wick. Your *vermin* aren't living up to expectations today."

"Careful, Becket," Cegrich said. "The game's far from over. I'll have that ball back and more."

I'll have your silence or your death, Cegrich wanted to say, but not here, not now. Becket's punishment for his hubris would come later, in a quiet, unassuming place, out of the way of probing eyes and investigating Enforcers.

Cegrich ignored Becket's muffled glee and watched his

team rally from the devastating loss of its star striker.

Every critical location within the sewage system was tracked through a series of interconnected vid screens. All images were piped into the coach's lounge, which was nothing more than a ten-by-ten hovel carved out of the base rock of the city foundation. From where he stood, Cegrich could safely watch all the action of the match. Those fans above the surface could watch as well at designated safe zones throughout the ruins and bid and haggle and argue over a game as necessary. The question on everyone's mind now was: who would win? Cegrich's Savage Nocturnals or Becket's Black Rock Killers? The answer to that question hung in the balance.

The Convict jack who had scooped up the bloody ball threw a short pass into the waiting glove of a Black Rock striker. The striker caught the ball with ease and dodged a Veer-myn guard whose mass propelled it through the foul runoff and into the central chamber wall. The striker then chose to flee down a main spoke toward Goal Two.

"He won't make it there alive," Cegrich said, letting his whip uncoil at his side. "Kaboom!"

"You forget, Cegrich," Becket said, folding his arms across his chest and flashing a satisfied smile. "We've played in this arena before. My boys know the pitfalls."

You may know the pitfalls, Becket, Cegrich said to himself, *but I own the bomb-maker and placer.*

The four main sewage lines that led from the central chamber were interlaced with smaller side tunnels that circled the entire Xtreme DreadBall arena like spokes on a wheel. If a main tunnel was blocked, the ball carrier could duck into a side tunnel and pop out in front of another goal, and potentially one that wasn't guarded by a castle or some cocky rookie who thought he could take on the world.

Cegrich loved this arena; he had played it multiple times. The humidity; the stench; the clutched, stifling atmosphere of it made him feel at home.

The Convict striker used the wide body of a guard teammate for cover, letting the heavily armored man mow a clear path that seemed promising at first, but quickly grew lousy with Veer-myn blockers intent on forcing his hand.

The Black Rock striker took the bait and ducked into a side tunnel. The screen in front of Cegrich switched to the new tunnel view. He watched and feigned concern for the benefit of Becket while he slipped his clawed hand into his robe pocket and quietly, carefully, clicked a button.

The signal went to a small shed above ground. There, a technician, whose job it was to randomly ignite bombs hidden beneath the loose bricks of the arena floor, clicked his own button. But, due to Cegrich's money, charming personality, and ability to hold family hostages, the technician sent the signal into the path of the charging Convict striker... and blew shards of eviscerated brick into his legs.

Oooo, how painful that must be, Cegrich thought, as he let a sheepish grin cross his rodent-like face and watched the wild ball fly out of the injured Convict's glove and ricochet down the tunnel.

It was Becket's turn to howl.

"Having been yourself incarcerated for over twenty years in a maximum security prison," Cegrich said with full satisfaction, "I would think you'd understand the vicissitudes of fate, *friend* Becket."

"Shut up!"

There was a death scramble for the ball, as players from both teams dove in to wrest it from its interminable bounce. A Convict who was part of the fray stepped on a pile of offal and slipped. He took a Convict jack and a Veer-myn guard down with him, and their collective weight snapped his leg. The man howled his agony to the joy of those watching on the surface. The Veer-myn guard, whose fall was cushioned by the Convict's bulk, grabbed the Convict's head and pushed it underneath the brownish-green liquid waste laying shin deep in the tunnel.

It was difficult to know which Convict guards wore shock or explosive iron collars. Becket changed them out every game and never bothered to share that information with his opposing coaches. Cegrich felt true anxiety now as he watched his guard hold the Convict's head below the foul muck, hoping the man would drown before an explosion occurred.

Becket angrily pushed his button, over and over again, screaming into the device resting in his withered hand. "Blow, blow!! Why won't you blow?"

Sometimes, Cegrich knew, collar bombs didn't explode as planned. He flashed a wide smile and stood there in rapt satisfaction as his star guard held the Convict's head below the rancid flow until the thrashing stopped.

The ball popped out of the fray, ricocheted off the wet, humid wall of the tunnel, and right into the glove of Cegrich's last striker.

"Run, run, you worthless Zee!" Cegrich screamed at the screen as it popped and sputtered due to the incessant heat and humidity of the coach's lounge. "Run!" He snapped his whip.

The Nocturnal striker did so, but not toward the closest goal at the sewer's second spill point. He ran back toward the central chamber and the waterfall.

A risky tactic, Cegrich knew, moving away from a close goal. But the striker understood well that the path to that goal was socked in with mad, embittered Convicts waiting to put their steel gauntlets down his throat and rip out his heart. Going in the opposite direction could take longer, but if the striker was smart enough and fast enough, he could be across the central chamber and into another main spoke, and on to Goal One without hindrance.

It became a chase as the Veer-myn crouched low and used his free hand to help propel himself faster across the wet, messy chamber floor.

From one of the few blind spots in the sewer that the cameras could not cover, a Convict jack appeared and slid across the chamber to try to undercut the Veer-myn striker.

"Get him!" Becket shouted. "Cut that Zwerm's feet out from under him!"

"Jump! Jump, you lousy rat!" Cegrich screamed in response.

The Convict jack slid hard across the chamber floor, splitting the toxic soup like the rudder of a boat, his steel-spiked boot set forward and ready.

The Veer-myn hopped just enough for the Convict to slip underneath him... but not quite high enough to miss a swipe from the jack's glove.

The electromagnetic scoop on the glove struck the Veer-myn striker's belly and rolled him up, over, and into the chamber wall, inches from the entry point of the main spoke leading to Goal One.

Another mad scramble for the ball ended beneath the waterfall as time ran out.

Becket's Black Rock Killers won by two.

Cegrich howled his rage and snapped his whip.

***

"It's my understanding that they call you The Whip?"

The human that called *himself* Manan stood before Cegrich in the central chamber, smiling the kind of insincere smile for which humans were notorious. He wore modest clothing, a loosely fitted tan pullover and simple black slacks. His hair was well-kept, his beard heavy but groomed. He was no First Sphere citizen, but he was not poor either.

Cegrich held the handle of his whip tightly and watched his team shower below the waterfall. A tap on the surface had been turned on, and so now clear, fresh water flowed into the sewer, ensuring that both teams cleaned up before emerging from the tunnels. *As if it made all that much difference*, Cegrich thought, as he sized up his visitor with his remaining good eye. The air above ground didn't smell all that much better than below. What could a simple shower accomplish?

"I have been called that, yes," he said, waving his whip around to catch the thin bars of light shining through gaps in the cracked concrete above. "And I've been known to use it a time or two on humans who waste my time."

Manan cleared his throat. "Then allow me to get right to it, Mr. Whip."

"You may call me Cegrich, if you prefer. It hardly matters either way."

Manan nodded. "Very well. I'm told, Cegrich, that you are a killer, that you know how to kill quietly and efficiently. Is it true?"

Cegrich grunted and barked a command at one of his players under the waterfall. The cowed jack grabbed a scrub brush and got back to it. "Who describes me as such?"

"Le Zuan Carooda."

Cegrich nodded and forced himself not to smile. "Oh, yes, Bossman Carooda. Interesting fellow. A pacifist. Wouldn't hurt a fly, though he employs people like me to do the kind of dirty shadow work that he refuses to do."

"How well I know," Manan said in agreement. "That is why I'm here. He refused to take the offer, but he recommends you highly. Please tell me his recommendation is sound."

"It is, if you had come to me a few years ago. These days, my time is spent coaching this sorry lot." He cracked his whip into the waterfall, though its steel tip missed flesh.

"Coaching and losing, it would seem."

On reflex, Cegrich almost turned and snapped his whip into Manan's face. But the human did not move, his expression never changing. He stared that condescending stare that humans often use against a Veer-myn when they are in a position of security and strength. This human had neither security nor strength. *How dare he come into my world and speak to me like this! How dare he!*

"You should know, Cegrich," Manan said, stepping forward through ankle-deep water, "that my client is well aware of where I am, and if I do not check in soon, they will come hunting for me. And I can assure you that my client has the resources to ensure that you never, ever, see the light of day, regardless of your history. And yes, I know you and your background, Cegrich. I know it well. So, I will ask you again. Are you the killer Le Zuan Carooda said you were?"

Cegrich gnashed his teeth to the point of pain. He had lost the game, and now he had to stand before this smug swine of a human and take this disrespect. In front of his players, no less. He could so easily flay this creature bloody and leave him to drown. *I can do it so easily...*

"Who is the target?" he asked.

"A human striker on the Vitala Vipers, goes by the name Jimbo Threpe. Mackinaw Jim, as the public knows him."

Cegrich searched his memory. "Yes, I seem to remember him. Pretty boy, flashy, good throwing skills. Why?"

Manan shrugged and shook his head. “He’s a means to an end.”

“What league?”

“The Vipers have just joined the FSIDL. Hope is their home planet. Regulation play begins soon. We want him dead before midseason.”

Cegrich nodded and considered. He shrugged. “Who is he to me? Hope is far away from our fairy garden here on Gaylor, and I’m sure it’ll be a fortress.”

“Don’t do it on Hope,” Manan said. “Catch him at an away game.”

“I respect your decision not to share your motives for this hit,” Cegrich said, stepping forward a pace and dragging his whip through the clear flow. “I ask in return that you not lecture me on how to do my business. I have a reputation and a position to uphold, here on Gaylor and elsewhere. The Whip doesn’t just go hunting for useless strikers. I’m not a thug, Manan, though you may think otherwise. I don’t waste my time on nobodies.

“If, however, your hit were more impactful to the GCPS at large, I might be inclined to accept. Such as... if the hit were against the Vipers coaching staff or its front office, I could be persuaded in that case.”

Manan sighed and shook his head. “Coaches Roth and Bock are not targets of this hit. They’ll be dealt with in other ways. We need you to—”

Cegrich put up his clawed hand. “Excuse me. Did you say ‘Bock’? As in, Carla Bullseye Bock?”

“Yes, that’s her. You know her?”

Cegrich nodded casually. “I’ve heard of her.”

He turned to his team. Many of them had moved out of the waterfall and were shaking themselves dry on the side. Two were still scrubbing themselves clean.

Cegrich cracked his whip, driving the steel tip into the backs of the two slow washers. "Move, damn you. Move! I will not tolerate lethargy on my team. Slowness kills. Slowness loses games. *Move... move!*"

Their backs flowed red, and Cregrich watched as the clear tap water turned a deep crimson. He stepped aside a meter to ensure their blood did not sully his leather foot covers. He breathed deeply. He closed his eyes and calmed himself by pulling his whip back and wrapping it in a loop over his arm. He breathed deeply again and turned to face Manan.

He smiled. "A hit against your Jimbo Threpe will require substantial payment," he said. "In advance."

Manan pulled a small device from his pocket and punched the clear screen several times. He then held the device up and showed Cregrich the number. "Is this sufficient?"

It was, but Cegrich hadn't been born yesterday, as they say. If the man was willing to pay that much without negotiation, he could go higher. "Double it," he said, "and you have a deal."

Manan punched more numbers into the device and offered it again to Cegrich. "Very well. We have a deal. Now, punch in an account number and half will be transferred immediately to said account. The other half when the deed is done."

Cegrich found it difficult to use the small device. His fingers were too long, claws too sharp to secure an adequate touch response when inputting data. But a little patience—in stark contrast to what he had just done to his poor players—worked well, and the funds were finally sent.

"I would stay longer, Cegrich," Manan said, bowing, "but I don't wish to be in your presence any further. I will go.

And remember. The name is Jimbo Threpe, and he plays for the Vitala Vipers. We expect to see him dead by game eight."

"Don't worry," Cegrich said, allowing the human to leave unhindered. "It'll be taken care of."

Yes, it would be. But not Mackinaw Jim. He was nothing. Less than useless. Nothing more than one of thousands of self-absorbed strikers strewn across the Spheres like stardust. Cegrich would make plans with the appearance that he was targeting Threpe. But Carla Bullseye Bock was his target now.

Just saying her name made his dry, scarred eye socket twitch with pain. She had taken away his eye, and now, he would take away her life.

Cegrich rolled up his whip and fastened it to his belt. He then led his team out of the sewer with a new spring in his step.

He had lost the game, yes, but he had won something far greater: the chance to right a terrible, terrible wrong.

I'm coming for you, Bullseye, he thought as the light of the surface spread across his face. *I'm coming for you.*

Chapter 5

Planet Hope, Viper Arena and Training Complex

Despite what it had been in a previous life, the Vipers' training facility now was more than Leeland could have asked for. In his mind, if memory served, it rivaled anything the Trontek 29ers had on their home planet, and perhaps it was even better, for it was newer. All the office space and cubicles and conference rooms had that new hover car 'smell,' as they say, and even though a large portion of the facility would probably never be used, Leeland appreciated that the FSIDL and Kapoor Industries had commandeered the entire facility. The excess space allowed him and his coaching staff to pick and choose what portions of the building would best accommodate their needs.

He picked the first floor for team training and game preparation. The locker rooms were on that floor anyway; plus, it provided better access to the team's weight room, equipment room, and training pitch. A short fifty-yard sprint through a tunnel put them into their home arena, which was technically a separate structure on the other side of the city block, with fan access from the adjacent streets and walkways. And last, but certainly not least, there was a first-floor kitchen fully stocked and in service when the team was not travelling to away games.

The second floor would be used for office space and media center. Leeland decided to make an altruistic gesture and give Aryan Kapoor the largest office on that floor. With their help, he then selected three offices for himself, Bullseye, and Conner that sat opposite the bossman's office.

In between were rows upon rows of empty cubicles that had yet to be removed. Leeland preferred it that way. It never hurt to have a barrier, even a flimsy one, between the coaching staff and the owner. Aryan had matured considerably since the end of the tournament, but he certainly wasn't mature or knowledgeable enough to involve himself into the minutia of DreadBall coaching. A lot of team owners put their noses in where they did not belong. Leeland wanted to make sure that that was not the case for the Vipers.

The third floor was designated as living quarters. The team would have to endure a central shower complex, but each person had his own room. There were even two guest rooms for MVPs that might be hired during the season. A circular hub of rooms with a centralized living and working space for the coaching staff had been set up as well. It was near the team rooms, but not adjacent, which again, Leeland preferred. Such a campus dorm room set-up would allow for him and his staff to meet in private and discuss matters on the fly without interrupting the team or having to go to their offices for every pertinent conversation.

The entire complex had been set up to function like a small, independent community, and Leeland was happy. The team and its organizational infrastructure were in place. Now all they needed to do was fill the last few remaining positions on the roster. Conner had moved quickly through the tryouts to secure signatures on contracts. The rest of the hopefuls were being put through a final set of rushes right now.

Leeland watched as his players went through their last full-contact practice. The only difference between an official DreadBall match and this was that the speed of the ball had been reduced to non-lethal levels. Leeland needed to see how well his team and potential hopefuls would play together, but he didn't need anyone getting seriously injured right before their first game against the Trontek 29ers.

Leeland had divided the Vipers into Red Team-Blue Team. They weren't treating it like a practice; they were hitting hard.

Little Frankie extended his glove and snagged the ball out of the air from a perfect Jimbo throw, only to be slammed into the pitch by Shadrack Menapi, who was playing in the opposing lineup. The ball spiraled out of Frankie's glove and bounced across the pitch. Spencer Mills on Blue Team tried catching it, but Caesar Maddog King undercut Spencer's legs and took him down. The ball continued to bounce as players on both sides fought for it.

Hopeful Kirkus Tetsudo, a relative unknown from a backwater Second Sphere League, finally scooped it into his glove with a perfectly placed electromagnetic pulse. He turned, made a slight shift to the left to avoid a slam from Jerold Minata, took another two steps into the closest strike zone, and launched the ball toward the goal.

Miss!

Jimbo was there to take the ball on bounce and then toss it to Little Frankie, who was down the field and pressing toward Blue Team's back goal.

"What do you think of Kirkus?" Conner asked as he and Leeland watched the scrimmage from Red Team's bench.

"He's got a good eye, good form, decent speed," Leeland said, "but he panics. There was no need to try that strike so quickly. He had plenty of room. He should have moved closer to get a better angle on goal."

Conner chuckled. "He's been taking cues from Jimbo: strike when you can."

"That works for Jimbo," Leeland said, "but not for everyone else. Kirkus has got to learn his own strengths and weaknesses, and then calibrate his play to his strengths."

Conner shrugged. "He's young, inexperienced, and nervous. But he's got the raw talent we need. I think he's worth signing."

"I agree, but we'll have to work on his decision making." Leeland looked down at the list of hopefuls on his tablet that were still under consideration. Most of them were on the pitch now or waiting to come in. Only one guard that they wanted was not present, and Bullseye was working on that. "Signing Tetsudo will leave us one striker, one guard, and two jacks short. Of the names on the list, who do you want?"

Conner took a while to answer, which gave Leeland additional time to watch the action.

Jimbo had scored from Kirkus's missed opportunity, so Red Team was up by two. The ball now resided in the hands of Artemis Hale, a Blue Team jack, with Shadrack plowing a good line to one of Red Team's front goals. Artemis was not what Leeland would call a consummate scorer; his skill was consistent with Conner's: he was better on defense. But at the moment, all of his Blue Team strikers were out of position and could not find an opening which would allow Artemis to toss them the ball. So, it seemed clear to Leeland that Artemis had decided to keep the ball and try to score on his own.

"Assuming that Bullseye is successful in her efforts and fills that final guard position," Conner said, "that would leave us with one striker and two jacks. Of the remaining hopefuls, I'd pick Rollin Peck for striker, Me-Shan Lo and Otis Chancey for jacks."

Leeland nodded. "Not bad choices, though I've not seen Me-Shan Lo play much."

Conner cupped his mouth with his hand and shouted, "Lo! Get in there!" He waved the jack in.

Me-Shan Lo was a small man, thin and wiry. When he had first arrived, Leeland had assumed that he was trying for a striker position, but not so. He took the field as a jack and was quite impressive at first glance. Incapable of delivering the kinds of slams that Conner preferred from his jacks, Me-Shan had the speed to rival any striker on the field.

Me-Shan took off after Spencer, who had acquired the ball on bounce after Artemis was slammed trying to score. Spencer was now trying to punch the ball into Red Team's back goal to put Blue Team up by one and end the scrimmage. Spencer was moving well, leaving Shadrack in the dust to question his life choices. The only thing that stood in his way now was Cyrus Voh, a new guard who had been signed just two days ago. Cyrus was a workman-like guard; competent at everything, great at nothing. Some might call him slam-fodder. Leeland despised the term but had to admit that everyone on a DreadBall team had his purposes. If it proved in time that Cyrus Voh's purpose was being slam-fodder, so be it.

Me-Shan, however, had no intention of allowing a showdown between Spencer and Cyrus. Catching up with Spencer within seconds, he moved into position and snatched the ball right out of Spencer's glove as if he were a striker. He then turned and raced back in the other direction, zigging and zagging his way through desperate, last second Blue Team lunges.

The buzzer sounded. The game was over. Red Team won by two because Me-Shan Lo stole the ball.

"I see what you're doing here, Conner," Leeland said, wagging an approving finger at his recruiter. "Suiting up a striker as a jack. Clever. Though it's going to become pretty obvious once we start playing that Me-Shan is out of position."

Conner returned the gesture with a sly smile and a wink. "Who cares, and what can they do about it? It's a rare, but not unprecedented, move. Never hurts to have additional scoring power on the field."

"You're beginning to think like a striker coach. I'm having an effect on you."

Conner smiled and winked. "Don't count on it."

In truth, Conner was beginning to think like a head coach, taking into consideration all facets of the game. It was good to see, but sad as well. Someday, Conner would mature professionally right out the door.

"Game over!" Leeland shouted over the pitch. "You men get cleaned up and get some food. Team meeting in two hours." He looked toward Me-Shan. He and Spencer were up in each other's business.

"Stand down, you two!" Leeland shouted as he considered moving onto the pitch and breaking it up physically. He thought better of it and repeated, "Stand down... now! It was a fair steal. Get over it, Spencer. Protect the ball better next time."

Me-Shan pulled away, and Spencer followed a few seconds later.

"Now *that* is what I'm most worried about," Leeland said, pointing toward the ended scuffle. "Big egos getting in the way of victory."

Conner nodded. "There's a lot of testosterone out there, Leeland. On any team, human or otherwise. But it'll be all right. If anyone can handle hotheads, it's you and Bullseye."

Just as he said her name, the door to Red Team's bench slid open, and Bullseye stepped in. She was in the one power suit she owned, a gold-red number to represent her official capacity as a member of the Vipers' coaching staff. Her face was radiant. Her eyes beamed.

"I take it that your trip went well?" Leeland asked.

"We got him!" She said. Leeland hadn't seen her smile that broadly in years. "Dillon Koch is ours."

Leeland leaned his head back and gave a satisfying sigh. "Good. Digby might rule against us on this, since he was technically under contract with the Jade Dragons."

Bullseye handed Leeland a tablet with the signed contract up and on full display. "Our lawyers seem to think that a clause in his contract gives Dillon the right to opt out prior to season start. They might challenge it; he may have to sit on the bench for a bit, but I think we'll win on appeal if it comes to that."

Leeland was almost as giddy as a schoolboy. He could hardly contain his joy. Getting the late Shyler Koch's younger brother to play in the final guard position was the stroke of luck he was looking for.

"I do, however, have some bad news."

And there goes the joy...

Leeland wiped his smile away with a frown. "What?"

"The Trontek 29ers just announced that they will be starting 'Lucky' Logan against us."

Jack and oftentimes team captain for the Trontek 29ers, it was assumed that Logan had not transitioned over to the FSIDL when the team had decided to join. A foolish hope, perhaps, but there had been no sign of him anywhere in any scouting reports the Vipers had received.

"What are we going to do?" Conner asked.

Not much we can do, Leeland wanted to say as he turned from Bullseye and stared out into the empty training space. He kept his mouth shut. Both Conner and Bullseye understood the situation as he did: there was nothing they could do about facing off against perhaps the best jack—the best human player—in the history of the sport. *All that we can do is face him and beat him.*

But how? Jacks, no matter how skilled, could be beaten. But Lucky Logan? He was something special.

Leeland considered, and considered some more. Then he got an idea, and his smile and joy returned.

"Get on the horn, Conner," he said, turning to his recruiter, "get on the horn, and get us Kreed."

Chapter 6

Planet Hope, Viper Arena and Training Complex

The rumors about Kreed were myriad and far-reaching, but over the years, a grain of truth had seemingly worked its way to the surface.

Without question, he was the tenth clone of Lucky Logan. The usual course of things had been that, when one Logan clone succumbed to injuries suffered on the DreadBall pitch, a new clone was created, thus ensuring Logan's legendary longevity.

Such a fate had not befallen Logan's tenth clone, however. As the rumors went, it had been sucked into a pocket dimension by the Koris en route to a frontier stadium, only to emerge years later a crazed, angry fellow with that proverbial chip on his shoulder. When he then saw Logan's eleventh clone playing DreadBall for the Trontek 29ers, he made it his mission to eliminate the 'imposter' and take back the life that had been rudely taken from him.

Whether or not all of these rumors were true, one immutable truth was clear to Leeland: Kreed was a fine DreadBall player.

"It's a risky move, Leelee," Bullseye said as they all gathered for their weekly team meeting. "Risky."

"If this were tournament play," Leeland said in a whisper so none of the players filing in could hear, "I'd agree with you. But this is league play. Our mission is to make a statement. To make it clear to the Trontek 29ers, and to anyone else, that the Vipers are here to play and not to be taken for granted. Kreed's a good player. Just as good as Logan, as far as I'm concerned. It'll work out."

"What clone is Logan on now?" Bullseye asked.

Leeland shook his head. "I don't know. Seventeenth? Eighteenth? I can't keep track."

They gathered in the team conference room on the second floor of the Viper complex. The room had an opulent feel to it, a half-moon shaped amphitheater with plush seating and all the modern technical amenities. The players found seats, and Leeland got to work.

"Quiet down!" he said. "Quiet down! Let's get started."

He allowed them to bring their rumble to a halt. Leeland took a moment to just look at the men on his team, all fourteen of their faces. Some he had known for a long time: Frankie, Shadrack, and Jimbo. Others—Kirkus, Dillon, and Me-Shan—he was just beginning to understand. At the beginning of any season, it was hard to know who on a team would excel, who would fail, who would die. It was the nature of the game, the nature of the business. The team that he and Bullseye and Conner had assembled was a good, solid group of players, more than capable of winning. But would they? And would all these faces be in the team meeting for the third or fourth game?

Probably not.

Bullseye cleared her throat, and Leeland snapped out of his trance. "Right. Yes, let's get down to it." He cleared his own throat. "I want to welcome you all to our first official strategy and tactics meeting."

"As if we had a choice in being here, right, Boss?"

Everyone laughed at Little Frankie's jest. Leeland smiled and nodded.

"Especially you, Frankie, judging by how you've been practicing of late." He winked at his rising star striker to another round of laughter. "Nevertheless, I welcome you all. We will take care of two orders of business today. First, I want to introduce you to Kreed. He'll be suiting up for our first game against the Trontek 29ers." Leeland activated the intercom and spoke into the mic quietly. "Kreed, will you join us, sir?"

A minute later, Kreed walked into the room.

The star jack looked like he had just rolled out of bed. His five o-clock shadow had a decidedly three-pm look about it. He wore purple sweatpants and a grey t-shirt. His famous abyss-black eyepatch was in place over his right eye. Leeland stared directly into the patch which covered a large portion of the ragged red scar running down the jack's face. Rumor had it that Kreed once killed a man for smiling while staring at his damaged eye. Leeland made sure not to smile.

Kreed walked across the room and stopped in front of Me-Shan Lo. "Slide over," he said, pointing to the left. It looked like the rookie jack was about to protest but thought better of it as Jerold Minata grabbed his sleeve and tugged him out of Kreed's way. Kreed sat, and Leeland continued.

"Thank you for joining us, Mr. Kreed." Leeland forced a smile. "Kreed's job in this game is to—"

"My job is very simple," Kreed said, interrupting. He snorted as if he were about to sneeze a massive ball of phlegm onto the floor. He swallowed instead. "If Lucky Logan and I are on the pitch at the same time, my mission is to kill him. Plain and simple. You boys go about playing your little game. I'll take care of Logan."

"I don't care whether you kill him or not, Kreed," Leeland said, beginning to reach the end of his patience. "As long as you keep him occupied, and you don't do anything that would otherwise jeopardize our ability to win."

Kreed stared at Leeland. Then he smiled and nodded curtly. "No worries... Coach. I'll earn my pay."

"I told you this was a mistake," Bullseye whispered behind him.

Leeland ignored her and continued. He tapped a few images on the tablet built into the podium he was standing behind, and a three-dimensional image of a DreadBall game flashed to life on a flat rectangular board to his right.

Tiny DreadBall players appeared in Trontek blue and Bremlin Nebula red. They moved up and down the bright black-and-white pitch that hovered a couple centimeters above the static board. The scene played out like a real DreadBall game, and some of the guys laughed at how comical such powerful, vibrant players looked in mini 3D. Leeland let the simulation run for several minutes. Then, he raised the pitch higher, switched the players from real images to red x's and blue o's, and paused the action.

"This was last season's playoff game against the 29ers and the Nebulas," Leeland said. "The 29ers won this game, and rather handedly. It tells us everything we need to know about where their team is right now and how to play them."

Leeland started the simulation again and let it run for another few minutes. One after the other, red x's winked off the pitch, until the Nebulas were well below six players and could not bring in any replacements. Then, Trontek's posture shifted from power to finesse. The tiny white ball dot was scooped off the pitch by a 29er striker who then slammed it into the back goal. Leeland paused again.

"See what they're doing?" Leeland asked. "They're playing like a Forge Father team. Power, power, power, until their opponent's Sin Bin is full of injuries. Then they strike. This is different than when I was on the team six years ago. Back then, we were all about scoring. Times change, leagues change, teams change. It's the nature of the business. So, we have to, as they say, fight fire with fire. We can't come out with a small lineup. We must meet muscle with muscle.

"We'll be started in a 1-3-2 lineup: one striker, three jacks, two guards. Exactly who will start in this configuration, we'll make that decision on game day. Although Kreed will be on the pitch if Logan is on the pitch. That's contractual."

Jimbo raised his hand. Leeland recognized him.

"Not to sound like I'm trying to wimp out or anything," Jimbo said, "but I recommend you start Frankie or Spencer. If I start, I guarantee that they'll try to knock me out right away."

"Oh, yes," Frankie said while rolling his eyes, "we can't afford to lose our *best* player, can we?"

"That's not what I meant," Jimbo said.

Leland jumped in before the matter escalated. "We'll cycle in more strikers as the game progresses. But we're going to start strong and go from there."

In truth, Jimbo's analysis was correct. He lacked the ability to articulate his reasoning, but it was sound. The first three or four rushes were always the most violent and kinetic in any match. Everyone on the pitch in those first few rushes was fresh and played with high energy. As the game progressed, players often grew tired and rattled, especially those returning to the game from the Sin Bin. At that point, bringing in a high scorer like Jimbo, well-rested and fresh off the bench, was ideal. It was a sound suggestion. Jimbo just didn't have the ability to articulate it without coming off as arrogant and self-absorbed.

Amidst a small amount of player chatter, the Vipers' newest guard, Dillon Koch, stood up.

"Yes, Dillon," Leeland said.

Dillon was a homunculus, the smallest, most perfectly formed human guard that Leeland had ever seen. He was shorter than Little Frankie, but he was as wide as a beer barrel and as muscular as Buzzcut. He was the brother of the late Shyler Koch, and even though he was the newest member of the team, the veterans all had great respect for him.

"I volunteer to start, coach," Dillon said, in his quiet, unassuming voice. "I know I'm new to the team, but I'm not a rookie. I can handle the 29ers. Put me in. I'll make plays."

Leeland nodded. "Thank you, Dillon. I appreciate your offer. But the lawyers are checking with Digby to ensure that you can actually start. If so, then I'll take your offer under advisement."

Dillon sat down, and Leeland continued. "One final thing I wish to point out. The Trontek 29ers play with a seventh man on the field. What do I mean by that? I mean their fans. They have the loudest, most loyal fans anywhere in the First Sphere. Hell, maybe in the entire GCPS. Maybe beyond. I know what I'm talking about. This will be an away game. We're going to be on their turf. It's going to get loud and rowdy. Don't let their seventh man intimidate you. Don't let him beat us. Any final questions?"

There were none, so Leeland ended the meeting.

As he was leaving, Leeland stepped in front of Kreed.

"Mr. Kreed," he said, feeling his heart race as he stared into the man's good eye. "I understand that we are contractually obligated to allow you to play off against Lucky Logan. I agreed to that, and that's what we want. But if you're on the pitch when he is *not*, I expect you to play Viper ball. You'll be suiting up in our uniform. As far as I'm concerned, you're a Viper, if for one game only. I expect you to play as a Viper."

Kreed stared at Leeland with his left, bloodshot eye. "Who are you to lecture me on how to play?"

Leeland was about to answer when Bullseye stepped to his side. "He's Leeland Roth and head coach of the Vitala

Vipers. If he can't impress upon you to behave... I will."

The standoff between Bullseye and Kreed broke records. As he waited for a break in their angry staring contest, Leeland's stomach growled. Finally, Kreed backed away and smiled. "No worries. I'll do my duty."

The star jack turned and walked away. Before he left the room, he hacked up a large gout of phlegm and spit it onto the floor.

"I warned you he'd be trouble."

Leeland nodded. "Well, Carla dear, if I'm proven wrong, it won't be the first time."

***

"Coach Roth, how does it feel to be returning to Trontek Stadium after all these years?"

"It feels fine. It was my home stadium for ten seasons. I know it; I think I still understand it. It's going to be a tough game, but a good game."

"Even though you will be, in effect, returning to the scene of a crime?"

That one stung, was disrespectful, and if the entire DreadBall community wasn't tuning in on this news conference, Leeland would jump over the podium and strangle the man. He flashed as sincere a smile as he could for the benefit of the viewers.

"I'll let history be the judge of any transgressions on my part. I'll say again what I've said many times before, however: I miss my brother. I think about him all the time, and if he were here today, I'd say to him how tremendously sorry I am for how things turned out."

Nearby, Bullseye scowled at the journalist who had asked that question. She too looked as if she wanted to throttle the poor fellow. Leeland tried changing the subject before things got out of hand. "Playing against the Tronteks at home is always a challenge. It's the greatest home field advantage in all the spheres. But we're up to that challenge."

"There are reports that Trontek owner and general manager Horus Ruth is planning to petition Digby to keep you from putting Kreed on the pitch. How do you respond to that?"

Leeland shook his head. "We have followed all the rules put forward by the governing body of DreadBall, and FSIDL, on signing MVPs to lineups. Horus Ruth may petition if he wishes; that is his right. But I'm confident that we'll be able to field the team we want to in a few days."

"What's it like coaching Kreed?"

"Challenging," Bullseye blurted from her seat.

Laughter, then, *"Coach Roth, there are reports that before he died, your brother Victor fathered two children and then abandoned them and their mothers. Can you confirm these reports for us?"*

Leeland furrowed his brow and shook his head. "Fanciful rumor. I know nothing about this, and I knew my brother well. He would never have done something like that."

"The report says that there were two children, one boy, one girl, but the truth of his affairs with their mothers was quashed in the press. In fact, the report says that Victor himself buried the truth from the public for fear that it would harm his career and his family's reputation."

"Ridiculous!" Leeland snapped. "Lies and fabrications. Look, people, if there are no further questions about our upcoming game, then this news conference is over."

Crickets... crickets... then, "Okay, that's all. Thank you all for coming."

Leeland and Bullseye walked out the back door and toward the stairwell. "I hate the press."

"I'm with you on that," Bullseye said. "That was a waste of time."

"All they ever care about is scandal and rumor. Conveyors of controversy. That's all they care about."

"Are the rumors true?" Bullseye asked. "About Victor?"

"Of course they aren't." Leeland stopped just before the stairwell. He sighed and rubbed his eyes. A headache surged behind his forehead. "I don't know. Maybe. We need to find out."

"Why?" Bullseye asked. "Victor's dead, and if true, it was many years ago. What does it matter now?"

Bullseye was right. At this point, it really didn't matter. Best thing to do was to simply allow the rumor to die on the wind. DreadBall would move forward as it always did, and within a couple weeks, the whole matter would be forgotten. But...

"*I* need to know," he said. "Victor was a lot of things, but I can't believe that he was a deadbeat father. Can you check into it, and let me know what you find?"

The look on Bullseye's face was something between shock and insult. "We've got a game to coach, Leelee. Remember? I don't have time to go looking into anything."

"Just contact Aryan and ask him to poke around."

"He's your brother. Why don't you—"

"Because if I'm discovered making that call, the press will jump all over it. If you make it, no one will care. No one will even bother to check it out."

Bullseye stewed in place. Finally, she said, "Fine. I'll make it. But you owe me big time."

Leeland smiled entered the stairwell. "Thank you, Bullseye. I always do."

Chapter 7

Trontek Arena

Rookie jack Artemis Hale was furious. "I bust my hump out there, Coach. I've earned a top spot. You're benching me?"

Leeland shook his head. "They're starting Logan. We've got to start Kreed. I believe I was very clear about our strategy in the team meeting."

"I'm a much better defender than Lucas or Jerold. Sit one of them."

"Relax, Arty. It's not like you won't have a chance to play. Trust me on this. The bodies will pile up quick."

Artemis scowled at his coach for a few seconds more, then fell in line with the rest of the team.

The roar of the Trontek crowd was muffled through the thick steel reinforcement walls of the tunnel in which they waited. In one minute, the doors would fly open, and the Vitala Vipers, the away team, would enter the pitch. The roar was muffled, but not the vibrations of the Trontek fans' incessant stomping. The floor shook. Leeland shook. Everything shook.

"I thought I was prepared for this," he said to Bullseye, "but I'd quite forgotten how raucous this place could be."

"Don't worry about it." Bullseye gave him a nudge. "We've got everything in place. We play our game the way we want, and we'll win."

No team that came into Trontek Arena ever played the game *they* wanted; not entirely, at least. "Is Conner up in the booth?"

Bullseye nodded. "Ready and waiting."

Conner would man the coach's booth and observe the game from above, thus giving Leeland and Bullseye a 'bird's eye view' of the action. Most teams assigned at least one of their coaching staff to such a role. During the season, either Conner or Bullseye would fulfill that obligation. Leeland would always stay on the floor.

Leeland shot a quick glance at his players who stood fidgeting behind him. Excited, anxious, their raw nerves were in full display on their faces and in the way they swayed back and forth in a kind of odd lockstep with the vibrations of the crowd. All but Kreed. He, in contrast, stood there like a rock, waiting, keeping his eyes fixed on the door. He almost seemed bored, but Leeland could tell that the superstar jack's mind was going a mile a minute. Through his poorly shaven face, his jaw muscles worked overtime.

"Ten seconds," a faint, but pleasant, female voice said over the comm.

"Get ready, boys," he shouted. "When these doors open, we'll be blinded by red light. It's a tactic. Close your eyes and wait for it to subside. Then move. Fast, furious. Take the pitch like you own it. No doubt. No fear. Fear kills in this arena."

"Five...four...three..."

Leeland closed his eyes. Bullseye squeezed his hand.

"Two...one..."

Boom!

The door opened, and sun-hot red light flooded in. Even with eyes closed, Leeland could feel the sting of the crimson glare and heat. "Steady...steady..." he shouted over the crowd whose roar was now at a decibel that hurt his ears. The sound was even more intense than he remembered it. "Steady...steady..."

The flash of red subsided. The heat bled away. "Now!"

He and Bullseye led the Vipers onto the pitch. He couldn't hear himself think. He didn't dare speak; no one could hear him if he tried.

They led the team into the arena through a whirlwind of sound and flashing red and blue and yellow and silver lights. Over the cacophony of screaming fans, a voice tried to introduce the Vipers and give their starting lineup. All Leeland could hear, as they assembled on the center line of the pitch, was the occasional name. Names that he hoped he'd be able to say again at the end of regulation. But seeing the mass of crazed fans screaming and shouting obscenities at them through thick ferro-glass barely protecting them from the mob, Leeland was not so sure. This was a set of fans that he had never seen in all the days that he had served the Trontek 29ers as a captain and lead striker. This was an angry, violent group. This was Horus Ruth's doing. There was no doubt of that in Leeland's mind.

A crowd bought and paid for.

He looked down the center line, taking stock of each of his players. He did not speak, but he could tell by their expressions what he would likely say.

Welcome to the big leagues, boys.

***

Hello, DreadBall fans, one and all! I'm Gregor Smoot, and you're watching SportsCam29. If you love DreadBall, and if you love the Trontek 29ers, then you're in the right place. Welcome to the Trontek Arena and game one of the third season of the FSIDL.

I'm contractually obligated to play it down the center, but if I had a choice, I'd have to go with the home team today. They'll be facing off against the new kids on the block, those intrepid serpents known as the Vitala Vipers, the first Third Sphere team accepted into the FSIDL. They're tough, no doubt about that, and with Leeland Roth as their head coach, I can only imagine what emotions might be going through their minds right now.

I was there at that fateful game six years ago when Leeland, then a star striker for the 29ers, killed his brother in what could only be described as a fit of anger. Now, Leeland is back and determined to prove something—perhaps to himself, to his brother, to the 29ers—perhaps even to me. But can he get out of this stadium in one piece? Listen to that crowd! The seventh man is definitely here and ready for blood.

Over the past couple seasons, the 29ers have bolstered their defenses, and now they field a team that can face off against any bruiser squad. Judging by its starting lineup, the Vipers will be doing much the same, matching strength with strength. Some might consider it a wise tactic. I guess we'll have to wait and see if it proves the right move for Roth and his snakes.

The teams are lined up, the ball cannon is ready. Let's get this game started...

***

As the ball rifled into play down the center line at one hundred sixty miles per hour, it was difficult for Little Frankie to ignore it. Reflexively, he stuck out his glove and unfurled his electromagnetic scoop to catch it, then remembered that that was not their play. Not initially, at least. He pulled his glove back just in time, and the ball flew past him toward the opposite wall. The ball was not relevant at the moment. What mattered was the wall of Trontek 29ers moving forward to engage.

Kreed moved immediately, caring nothing about the ball. His eyes were fixed on Lucky Logan, who had held himself back a few paces from the center line. A Trontek guard moved to intercept; Kreed ducked and let the lumbering brute stumble past as if he had stubbed his toe on a rock.

Logan, seeing his clone bearing down on him, instead chose to go after the ball, which had struck the wall and had ricocheted into the Vipers' side of the pitch.

The rest of the players on both teams struck in the middle.

Leeland watched the opening moves from the Viper bench, giving deference to Bullseye's direction. Going with a defensive lineup meant that she and Conner had the reins, at least right now. Later, when more strikers took to the pitch, Leeland would chime in.

In pre-game prep, Bullseye had instructed her starting guards Shadrack and Dillon to 'lock it up' with their two opposing Trontek guards. They had followed her instructions to the letter and were now facing off against their marks, trading blows for blows, and circling each other in a kind of comical two-step. But the kind of punishment they were exchanging was no laughing matter, and Dillon, his center of gravity lower than anyone else's on the pitch, put a strong uppercut into the sternum of his Trontek guard and put him down.

A medibot flew onto the pitch and pulled the injured 29er guard to its Sin Bin.

A scoring lane for the Vipers opened.

Unfortunately, the ball had scattered into Viper territory, far away from any Trontek strike zones. Four players scrambled for it.

Three, plus Kreed. His mind was still fixed on taking Logan down. He was moving so fast that his body was nothing more than a streak of Viper red and gold, but both Leeland and Bullseye saw the sharp object peeking out of his glove in the glint of arena blue light.

"He's got a weapon," Bullseye said.

Leeland nodded. "Yep. Replaced his EM scoop with a retractable blade with casing that looks like a launcher. I noticed it before we fielded."

"He'll be kicked out of the game."

He smiled. "Only if he gets caught."

Leeland was more than happy to allow Kreed to live up to his reputation. If the MVP wanted to use dirty tactics, weapons, so be it. This was league play... and this was Trontek. This was war.

Little Frankie and Trontek star striker Mattis Rakoczi worked to claim the ball. They bounced off each other like asteroids in a belt. Each was as fast as the other, but Rakoczi was more skilled and more able to deal with the pulsing lights and raucous crowd. Leeland could tell that the seventh man was affecting his striker's concentration. They were mere feet away now from the ball, but Rakoczi had the inside lane. His long, blue scoop pulsed out of his glove and snatched the titanium sphere before it could strike the wall again. Frankie tried to steal it, but his inertia took him past Rakoczi and out of position.

Fortunately, the Trontek striker was out of position as well and could not move to put himself into a strike zone before Viper jacks Jerold and Me-Shan Lo would reach his position.

But there was Lucky Logan, living up to his name. Standing all by himself near the Viper back goal; a clean three-point opportunity. Rakoczi shoveled the ball to Logan with an underhand flick before being crushed under the weight of the Viper jacks.

Logan caught the ball, turned quickly, and tossed it into the goal.

Score!

The arena erupted. Kreed slammed into Lucky Logan's back and rode him all the way to the wall.

Ooooh! What a hit! Logan's luck just ran out. My, my, my, my, my. I don't think I've ever seen such a strike in all my days. Wait! Something's amiss near Kreed. The cyber-referee is looking into it. The Eye in the Sky has turned its ocular bulb toward the spot. Wait... wait... no, nothing. Looks like the ref didn't find anything. It was a legal shot, though, and with Kreed, you can never be sure.

The 29ers are up by three, but they're in trouble. Three players out that first rush. Can they pedal back and defend their goals? The ball's back in play. Let's find out...

Lucky Logan was removed from the field, and now Kreed had a free hand.

The ball popped into play again, ricocheted off Dillon Koch's armor, and this time, bounced into the Trontek side of the field.

Down by three, there was an immediate feeling of panic among the Viper players on the field as Little Frankie and Me-Shan Lo scrambled for the ball. Seeing, and perhaps even feeling, their anxiety, Bullseye screamed from the sidelines, "Work the game plan. Work the plan! Don't panic. Hit those sons of Zees!"

Shadrack and Dillon recommitted to the plan, moving accordingly to shadow any and all Trontek guard movement on the pitch. Near the middle of the center line, a scramble for the ball was forming, as Trontek players, over-excited by being up by three so early in the game, forgot their plan of attack and tried snagging the ball. Shadrack dove into the pile and knocked two Trontek jacks from the fight. Doing so knocked the ball further into 29er territory.

Kreed, moving even faster than Little Frankie, blew past the mob and reached for the ball, then suddenly realized that he couldn't catch it due to his little hidden weapon. Instead, he batted it to the left with his glove, pretending, for the benefit of the referee, to have stumbled upon the attempted catch. Little Frankie was there waiting.

He scooped the ball into his glove and dodged a slam from a Trontek jack. He looked toward the back goal. It was open, and Me-Shan Lo was waiting for a toss. But fresh Trontek players were coming onto the pitch to replace the injured, and so he didn't feel confident with his throw. Instead, he stepped three paces left and slammed the ball into the goal, bringing the Trontek score down to two.

"Jimbo would have made that toss," Bullseye said.

Leeland nodded. "True, but a score is a score."

The ball was shot back into play.

Mattis Rakoczi, just returning from his initial slam, moved to intercept. Shadrack stepped into the striker's path, knocked him up into the air, and then onto his back. A wicked slam, indeed, but Rakoczi appeared to be only dazed. Then Shadrack was hit by a Trontek guard and jack. He struck the floor and didn't move.

Another titanic hit! Wow, I'm not sure there's going to be anyone left alive by end of regulation. There's another scramble for the ball, but half the players on the field don't seem to care. Look at those fists fly!

"Maddog," Bullseye shouted as Shadrack's limp body was dragged off the pitch. "Get in there!"

Caesar Maddog King blew through the entry point. Living up to his moniker, he dashed across the pitch and flew into the scramble for the ball.

"He knows he can't actually catch the ball, right?" Leeland asked. "He understands a guard's role, right?"

Bullseye couldn't help but laugh. "He understands, Leelee. He's just trying to get his gloves wet with Trontek blood. A pile on for the ball is the best place to find fresh meat."

Leeland's earpiece pinged, and Conner's voice came through from the coach's box. "Lucky Logan is coming back in."

Leeland blinked twice. "Already? Kreed knocked him into the Second Sphere."

"They don't call him Lucky for nothing," Conner said. "Also, tell Bullseye I recommend we go into castle immediately."

"Why?" Leeland asked. "If we do that, we'll have to move to an offensive stance. It's too early."

"Trust me on this one, Leeland. I've good intelligence that the 29ers are just going to keep hitting the back goal. They actually don't care if they lose. They want to hurt us. Horus Ruth wants to hurt us. They'll make it look good for the press and for the fans by trying to hit the back goal as often as possible, but they're not wasting time on petty one-pointers back and forth. Cover the back goal now, and force them into a different policy."

"Where'd you get this so-called 'good intelligence'?"

"A little bird named Shapshir Goethe sang it to me."

Leeland was beginning to love and hate their Asterian liaison. Love because of his seemingly rock-solid loyalty to his team. Hate because the acquisition of such 'intelligence' could get them in trouble with Digby. There was no specific rule that said that a team could not utilize off-pitch information to better its position in a game. But such practices, if they became public, could cause a distraction that a team didn't need, especially one like the Vipers who were trying to make it in a top shelf league like the FSIDL. To be thought of as a team that must cheat to win games can be a debilitating situation.

Leeland clicked off his comm. "Conner says to form a castle."

Bullseye leaned away from Leeland as if he had just farted. "Castle? So early? That'll force us to change our plan."

Leeland waved off her concern. "Just... do it. It's my call."

Bullseye stretched her neck. "You're the boss."

What's this? Leeland 'I Hate Castling' Roth is forming a castle? Well, perhaps that's Carla Bock's influence. Not a bad strategy, but let's see how it plays out.

Bullseye gave the sign of castle to Dillon, and he and Me-Shan and Maddog back-pedaled from their positions near the center line. It was more of a slow fighting withdrawal, as, with each step backward, they were shadowed by Trontek jacks and guards determined *not* to let them castle. Meanwhile, Kreed took advantage of the clearing center and went after Lucky Logan.

This time, Logan seemed just as determined to meet Kreed. They struck in the center.

They locked arms. Kreed tried getting a shot with his tiny hidden blade into Logan's armpit, where the armor was weakest. But he and Logan had met on many occasions, and his adversary was ready for it. Logan grabbed Kreed's arm and tried to turn the tables by pushing the blade back into Kreed's side. Their helmets struck, and although their faces could not be seen due to their visors, Leeland could imagine the hateful words they might be using.

The ball flew by, and a mass of men followed.

For a moment, Leeland noticed that Kreed seemed to consider breaking off and giving pursuit—it was written in the DNA of every DreadBall player to follow the ball—but Logan made a mistake. He lifted his left arm to try to deflect the raging titanium sphere. Kreed attacked, punching his blade into Logan's side, again and again, until he must have felt and heard the meaty slice of skin and bone. Logan dropped to his knees. He tried wrapping Kreed's legs, and for a moment, Kreed wobbled as his right knee gave under Logan's grasp. But he quickly recovered his strength and raised his blade to deliver the final blow.

The Eye in the Sky beamed red light onto Kreed's blade. Klaxons sounded. *"Kreed! You are in possession of an illegal weapon. You are eliminated from the game. Cease your attack and leave immediately!"*

Kreed did not listen. He continued to drive his blade into Logan's side while the life continued to drain out of him.

"Get off the pitch, Kreed!" Leeland shouted from the sidelines. "It's over!"

The man had done his duty, and there was no reason for him to remain. But Kreed hadn't come to follow Leeland's orders or anyone else's. His mission in life was to kill Lucky Logan, and that's what he intended to do. But no player can ignore the Eye in the Sky when it orders him or her off the pitch, especially in the Trontek arena.

Three security drones flew into the arena. They created a triangle around Kreed and shot him with electrical bolts.

One, two, three, each shot striking a different place on his armor. Kreed stood there, taking each shot, jerking as if he were being electrocuted which, in truth, he was. The shots stopped, and he fell. Leeland could almost smell Kreed's burning hair and beard. He shook his head.

"Well, his day is done. But so too is Logan's. I can't imagine anyone coming back with those wounds." He turned to the bench. "Artemis... your turn."

Artemis stood, slapped on his helmet, and entered the arena.

Three rushes later, with the 29ers still up by two, Little Frankie went down.

"Jimbo, you're up!"

The game now turned to offense, as both teams shifted to a lighter lineup to focus on scoring.

Jimbo Threpe took the ball on a toss from Me-Shan Lo. A Trontek jack tried sweeping his legs, but Jimbo leaped at the right time and left the man in shock. He was his arrogant self out there, playing loose with the ball, playing to the crowd which wanted nothing more than to see the great Mackinaw Jim ground into dust. Jimbo smiled, waved at them, and took it all in, drawing strength from their anger, their contempt.

"He is a showman," Leeland said to Bullseye over comm. She had moved over to the Sin Bin to check on Shadrack. "Let's hope he gets the job done."

"Tell him to stop playing and put the ball in a goal," she replied, and Leeland could hear Shadrack cursing the striker in the background.

Conner chimed in. "Tell him to head to the far left goal and take a two-pointer. Looks like the 29ers are having trouble securing all three goals right now."

"Why not the back goal then?" Leeland asked.

"Take a look."

Leeland raised up on tiptoes and saw what Conner was alluding to.

Lucky Logan was back on the pitch. *Impossible! How could this be?* But there he was, now part of a castle being formed to block any three or four point tries. Was this the same Logan? Number seventeen? Number eighteen? Perhaps the 29ers had fresh Logan clones standing in line, like uniforms on pegs in a locker room. A never-ending supply. *Ridiculous! You can't win against this guy!*

"They're willing to play to a draw," Conner said, "and beat us in overtime. Go for the draw."

Leeland jumped to it, pointing Jimbo to the far Trontek zone. There were hazards in the way, but Jimbo saw his coach's hand signal and moved accordingly, ducking a mighty roundhouse from a guard and then protecting the ball from a pesky striker who tried picking his pocket. Maddog broke away from the castle and ended that theft attempt by putting the 29er striker face first on the pitch. Then he tried clearing a path to the two-point strike zone but was undercut by an angry 29er jack who was called for a foul and ordered off the pitch.

Jimbo moved through the mass of twisted, contorted bodies, wailing fists, and cracked helmets. Like a dove among cats, he seemed impervious to the claws around him. The path before him parted like water against a rudder, and he took no time in reaching the strike zone.

He slid into the two-point position, paused a critical second for effect, and then rifled the ball toward the goal.

The crowd stopped its screaming and stomping. Lights stopped flashing. Horns stopped blowing. And perhaps it was the sudden cessation of all those things—the sounds, the colors, the vibrations—that put the ball just a tad off to the left. Its speed was adequate, but its angle was sharp.

The ball struck the goal, bounced twice, and dropped out. The endgame klaxons sounded.

The Trontek 29ers won by two.

Chapter 8

Planet Hope, Viper Arena and Training Complex

Leeland was not upset with a first game loss. Granted, a loss was a loss, and with so few games in the season, it could come back to bite them in a tender place. But the Vipers had played well, had weathered the seventh man, and had come up just short. Kreed's contribution was not decisive, but Leeland figured that keeping Logan occupied had probably contributed to the low, but close, score, and the 29ers inability to achieve an early victory. No one had come out of the game with serious season-ending injuries. No one had been killed. All in all, it was a good game, a good start.

The only problem was having to play therapist to Jimbo.

"I want to apologize again, Coach," Jimbo said in Leeland's office as they waited for Bullseye to arrive. "I screwed that up."

Leeland sighed and rubbed his face. "How many times do I have to say it, Jim? Let it go. You missed a shot. It happens."

"Yes, but I never miss."

Leeland wagged a finger. "Not true. Your career average is eighty percent, which is phenomenal, but not perfect. You've missed strikes before. Get over it, or I'm going to punch you in the face." Leeland cracked a smile and winked. "Jim, I need you focused on our next game against the Pelgar Mystics. You're going to start. Do you understand me?"

Jimbo nodded. "I understand. I've never played against Judwans before."

Leeland was surprised. "Never?"

"Never. I'm not sure why, but there it is. I hear they play mind tricks on their opponents."

"Yes. We've nothing physically to fear from them; Judwans are pacifists and therefore rarely slam, if ever. It'll be a totally different game than the one we just played. They mess with your perception, your subconscious. They move in very rhythmic patterns, confusing their opponents as to their exact locations on the pitch. That's why I need your mind sharp, Jimbo. Stop coming in here and apologizing."

The despondent striker nodded.

Bullseye entered the office. The look on her face was not what Leeland wanted to see.

"Jimbo," Leeland asked, "can you go and gather all the strikers together? I'll meet you guys on the training field in about thirty minutes."

"Sure thing," Jimbo said, picking up his sparkling cane—more for show than walking—and departed. Bullseye patted him on the shoulder as he left.

"Give me good news, Carla," Leeland said, taking to his chair and falling into it as if he were sliding into a pillow. He certainly needed the rest.

"I wish I could," she said, finding her own seat, "but it's bad and even worse. Which do you want first?"

"Let's start with the deadbeat charge. Is it true?"

Bullseye nodded. "Victor had two children. DNA scans have just been concluded and confirmed. The boy and his mother died in a shuttle accident on travel back to the mother's home planet. That was three years ago. The other mother and his daughter are still alive, and..." she seemed very hesitant to continue "...the mother's having a press conference later today to confirm for the public that Victor Roth was the father."

Lovely! If there were something heavy lying on his desk right now, Leeland would have picked it up and thrown it against the far wall. Only papers, game play worksheets, diagrams, and his and Conner's work tablets covered the teakwood surface. He wasn't about to throw his own tablet, and he'd never hear the end of it if he chucked Conner's. No, he'd have to be content with just throwing his arms in the air.

"Okay, my brother sired children and abandoned them. It's personally painful, insulting. I thought he was a more honorable man than that. But I don't see how this impacts me, or us, in any meaningful long-term way."

"Some are saying that the mother is holding the press conference in an attempt to extort money from you," Bullseye said, "seeing as you are the only living member of the Roth family. And you're rich."

Leeland huffed. "Rich by DreadBall standards, which as we can see here on high corporate Hope, doesn't amount to much. It depends on whether she's honorable or not. If her intention is extortion, that'll become clear very quickly."

Silence fell between them as Leeland sat and contemplated the situation. A distraction, and personal disappointment, indeed; but as he had said, not something that should impact him or the team moving forward. Yet, he couldn't help but wonder who these women were, who their children were. The deaths of one mother and Victor's son—Leeland's apparent nephew—were terrible. But what of his niece? Who was she? What was she like? What did she look like? He hoped that the mother had enough integrity not to exploit her daughter and parade her in front of the media as it swarmed like sharks in bloody water.

"Want to hear the bad news?" Bullseye asked.

Leeland shook his head. "No."

Bullseye breathed deeply. "The *Hope Sentinel* is going to release a report today claiming that Victor was involved with Rebs in a money laundering scheme."

"Total crap!"

She nodded. "I contacted a few of my marine pals still working the scope, and they can't confirm it. It seems like a thin charge—"

"Because it's a lie."

"—but nevertheless, it's going to be out there soon." Bullseye leaned back in her chair. "Another controversy the press is going to hit us on."

"They can hit us all they want," Leeland said. "I'll deny that load of garbage to the end of my days. My brother may have left children behind, but I guarantee he did not conspire with Rebs. He was more of a corporate loyalist than I."

He stood. What a ridiculous charge, and one that wouldn't go far. So, the only reason to flash it on every news vid throughout the First Sphere was to damage reputations, to distract, to cause short-term harm. *To me and to the Vipers.* Leeland could only think of one person who was cruel enough, vindictive enough, for such an act.

"Have you spoken with Aryan yet?"

Bullseye shook her head. "No, he hasn't responded."

"Don't worry about it, then. If he calls, take the call, but if not, I'll get a hold of him."

Leeland walked to the door and opened it. "Wait," Bullseye said. "Where are you going? I thought we were going to discuss the next game."

"We will, today. Right now, I'm going to go teach my strikers how to beat monks."

And to blow off some steam...

***

Today's practice would be positional. Strikers now, guards and jacks later. Leeland was the Vipers' head coach, but he also served as their striker coach and offensive coordinator. During the Third Sphere tournament, there had been little time for personal attention. League play was quite different.

First up: catching the ball. Strikers, the chief ball-handlers on the pitch, needed constant practice to maintain their skills and sharp edge. Leeland lined them up on the center line and then had his practice staff fire balls at top speed at his strikers. Little Frankie was first up, then Jimbo, then Spencer, Kirkus, and finally their newest rookie, Rollin Peck, who seemed afraid of the ball and tried to catch it by fully extending his arm and electromagnetic scoop like a stick poking a poisonous snake. The rookie deflected more passes than he caught. After about half a dozen misses, Frankie and Spencer taught the boy how to catch properly. By the end of that session, Rollin was catching about seventy-five percent of tosses.

Next up: scoring. Jimbo became the coach; Leeland advised.

They huddled on the center line. "The key to effective scoring," Jimbo said, "is vision. The speed of the ball coming off your launcher will do its job. Don't worry about trying to put too much spin or thrust into the toss. Doing so will inevitably force the ball off target."

"Jimbo's right," Leeland said. "Let the glove do its job. Your job is to see the goal and release at the right moment to ensure that that little titanium bulb hits the right spot."

"My recommendation," Jimbo said, "is to never try to arc the ball into the goal. It can work sometimes, but it's not a viable option in most cases. The game is too fast, too brutal, bodies moving in and out of your vision too quickly. A straight shot on goal is your best option. And here's how you do it."

Jimbo caught a ball rifled into play. He then moved straight toward the back goal at a casual pace, this time not bothering to play to a crowd that didn't exist, although it seemed to Leeland that his star striker had to restrain himself not to wave out of habit. Jimbo finally reached the four-point spot on the back strike zone, raised his arm, and fired the ball straight into the goal. Perfect.

"Now," Jimbo said, "you score like this by releasing the ball just as your arm becomes level with the goal. It's a split-second decision that requires good vision. You have to see, almost feel, the exact moment when your glove is at the right spot for launching. But if you do, I can almost guarantee you'll score."

There were a million tiny little things during a game that determined success or failure in a score attempt, Leeland knew. He was at least glad that Jimbo left some wiggle room with 'almost guarantee.' A DreadBall match is never won or lost strictly by the numbers.

"Also remember that the closer you are to the goal," Leeland added, "the better your chances of scoring. You all know as well as I do that, in reality, DreadBall is a low-scoring game. Blowouts are rare. Not impossible, but rare. So, unless time is running out and you *must* strike the goal at the furthest strike zone point, step a few paces forward, and give yourself a better chance."

For the next thirty minutes, they practiced scoring. Jimbo observed and mentored. Frankie's strikes on goal had improved tremendously since the Third Sphere tournament, although he still seemed a little hesitant at releasing the ball.

Too many marbles were rolling around in the lad's head, Leeland knew. That was the joy of a player like Jimbo Threpe: he never let his mind get in the way of his natural talent. Frankie was a thinker, and that skill could prove decisive in a game. But for straight scoring, that was best left to guys like Jimbo and now, apparently Kirkus Tetsudo, who was showing tremendous ball handling and scoring skills. Not as accurate as Jimbo, but in the course of practice, Kirkus was consistently striking three- and four-point goals at a higher percentage than anyone else. Leeland was pleased with the young man's improvement and made a note on his tablet to start him with Jimbo in the next game.

The session concluded with agility training. Each striker was required to weave his way across the pitch by maneuvering around a series of electromagnetic shields that randomly popped up from the floor. The strikers were then required to make split-second decisions on how and which direction to dodge the shields. It wasn't easy.

It took Jimbo three tries to reach the back goal. On the second try, he was smacked back so hard by a shield appearing right in his lane that it seemed as if he wouldn't be able to complete the session. But on the third try, he reached the back goal and scored. Frankie made it on his second try but did not score. Spencer, the same. Kirkus made it on his final try and managed to slam the ball home. Rollin didn't even make it, though he did manage to place one foot in the back goal right before a shield flew up in his face and knocked him out cold. Leeland snickered from his observation point; the medibot who came on to drag Rollin away looked to do the same. The poor boy was trying, at least, and in practice, that was all Leeland asked of his players.

Practice ended for the strikers. Conner and his crew of jacks came on the pitch to take over. He and Leeland stopped to chat.

"How goes it, Boss?" Conner asked.

Leeland nodded. "Pretty good. Rollin isn't ready to start yet. He'll be warming a bench for a while. Otherwise, not bad. Scoring percentage and ball-on-goal percentage is up as well. We'll need those kinds of numbers against the Mystics."

"I'm thinking it might be wise to bring in a Mu'Shen'Wan priest or two for practice," Conner said, "pulling their feints and misdirection on our players as they go through their drills. Just to get them acquainted with the kind of mind tricks that the Judwans practice during games."

"I wish you had recommended that strategy beforehand," Leeland said. "We've no time to employ such folk now."

"No, not for this first game. But for our second game against the Mystics later in the season, we do."

"Very well. Check out our options. I'm sure there's a Judwan monk or two around that would be willing to work with us, for the right price."

Leeland's comm pinged him.

"The press conference has started," Bullseye said. "You want me to watch it, give you details later?"

"No. You work with your guards, get them ready for the Mystics. I'll check it out in my office."

***

She was a beautiful child, eight years old, and a spitting image of Victor. She and her mother were greeted warmly by the press, and then the girl was ushered offstage before the conference began.

Eight years old? That meant she was at least two when her father had died. *Did my brother ever see his daughter?*

The mother made an opening statement. "I am not here for money or for celebrity. I've no intention of extorting or suing anyone for monetary gain. I simply want the truth to be known. Victor Roth is the father of my daughter, Victoria."

She was then bombarded by questions, both reasonable and cruel. *How can you be sure Victor Roth is the father*? one reporter asked, as if he were living in ancient times and not the modern GCPS with all of its available technology to trace genetic lineage. *What do you think Victor's motives were for keeping your relationship secret? Why didn't you come out sooner? Why now? When your daughter comes of age, do you plan on letting her choose her surname? Is your daughter doing well in school? Do you intend on reaching out to Victoria's uncle, Leeland Roth, who...* on and on and on it went, and despite Leeland's anger that this truth about his brother was coming to light, he couldn't help but feel sorry for, and admire, this woman who was the center of attention on the vid screen in front of him. She was cool, collected. She answered every question with an articulation that meant either she had been well-coached beforehand, or she was just a natural born speaker, communicator. Every arrow slung her way, she flung right back, until the press was left with no more arrows in their quiver, no more bolts in their pistols. An hour later, the conference ended, but one question still lingered in Leeland's mind. Perhaps she had said it before the conference had begun; perhaps she had said it during the conference and he had missed it, so wrapped in thought. But...

What is the woman's name?

His comm pinged. "Yes, what is it, Shapshir?"

The Vipers' liaison to the front office seemed hesitant to explain why he had called. "The press would like to have a word with you, Leeland. Just five minutes?"

Leeland shook his head, though he knew the Asterian could not see him. "No. I'm giving no one five minutes today. I've a game to prepare for. Any questions they may have about today's press conference, I'll answer in the normal course of time, per usual."

Leeland cut the link and leaned back in his chair. He breathed deeply then let it out slow and steady. He closed his eyes and tried to deliberate on strategy and tactics. Game two was on their doorstep. The Pelgar Mystics. But all he could think about was the image of the girl, his niece, and her mother, just as beautiful as her daughter, and so very skilled at...

What is her name?

Chapter 9

Pelgar Mystics Stadium

The glass dome of the Pelgar Mystics' new stadium was a marvel in engineering. It functioned like a kaleidoscope when the panels of the top portion of the dome rotated clock and counter-clock. The colors reflected onto the pitch and throughout the bleachers from this rotation had a soothing, almost mesmerizing, quality. Fans attended live games just to find peace from their daily grind. It was the kind of therapy that Le Zuan Carooda needed in his life.

"I've heard that at least seventy-five percent of all attendees fall asleep before the final rush," Manan Kapoor said as he and Carooda watched the game from the Judwan gangster's sky box. It, too, was glass, and reflected aesthetically pleasing light onto the thick shag carpet.

"I'm surprised it's so low," Le Zuan said, breathing in the manufactured air filled with the scent of lilac and rosemary. "It doesn't matter if the fans fall asleep while watching. What matters is if the opposing team does."

"Does it work?" Manan asked.

Le Zuan shrugged. "Sometimes."

Four rushes into the match, and the Vitala Vipers were up by two.

"They play well," Manan said. "Kapoor Industries made a good investment."

Le Zuan grunted. "On the team itself, or Leeland Roth specifically?"

"Are the two mutually exclusive?"

Arrogant human! Le Zuan thought as he sampled a small snifter of wine on the table near his right hand. It had a good, rosy flavor. A little wood. A tad too sweet for Le Zuan's taste, but a reasonable vintage at a reasonable price. A human Corporation blend. At least humans were good for something.

Manan cleared his throat. "I'm surprised that you would attend this game, given your... involvement in the matters pertaining to Victor Roth."

Le Zuan chuckled, a high-pitched squeal/whistle that clearly annoyed Manan's human ears. "There is absolutely nothing wrong with a businessman like me coming to the game and enjoying a pleasant afternoon in the warm, therapeutic sun. Besides, I used to be a member of this team, remember? And, as I have said, I am a pacifist. But I've learned over the years that, in order to maintain a tight grip on the emotions that can erupt into violence, it's wise to remember what violence looks like, lest we forget. What better way to remember than by watching a DreadBall match?"

Manan had no return for that. Le Zuan finished his wine and settled back to watch the game.

The Mystics scored, evening the game. The Viper fans—though few—booed and carried on in their dissatisfaction at the turn of events, while the Mystic fans remained stoic and respectful. Pelgar bodies flew onto and off the field as Viper slams mounted. The reason the score was so close was because, despite their flare for brutality, the Vipers couldn't handle the lithe, mesmerizing moves of the Judwan strikers. They were so confusing to the small minds of the human players that nearly every time a Viper striker tried to score, he'd get his pocket picked, and the chase would be on. So, all in all, it was a good game with just the right amount of blood and meditation.

Seeing humans beat up on his Judwan brethren was also a reminder of his people's struggle against the GCPS.

What better way than to see the physical manifestation of Judwan oppression than on a DreadBall pitch? It made him angry, and anger turned into money, money into action, action into—

"The news has been good of late," Manan said, lifting his wine snifter in salute.

Le Zuan nodded. "It's only beginning. By the end of the season, Leeland Roth and his Vipers will be swimming in controversy."

Manan saluted again. "I thank you."

Le Zuan didn't bother recognizing the man's second thanks. He turned back to the game and watched as Jimbo Threpe took the ball on a bounce and moved to score.

Threpe was an impressive human striker. Not quite as agile as a Judwan, and like most humans, his self-absorption poured out of his body like foul sweat. But he had a good eye and good instincts. He moved through the tangle of Mystic strikers as they clawed at his arms to try to strip the ball. Help from a Viper guard and jack pushed the Judwan pile out of the way and gave Threpe an open lane. The human striker slid into the closest strike zone and shot the ball into the goal.

And just like that, the Vipers were up again by two.

"He's impressive," Manan said. "It almost feels like a crime to put such a talented man down."

Manan's attempt at assassination humor was lost on Le Zuan. It wasn't very good humor. "I wouldn't lament about such things out loud, Manan. One must have faith that all will be right with the universe in the end. There is a lot of DreadBall left to play this season." Le Zuan poured himself another snifter. "Now, let's sit back and enjoy the end of the game."

And when would Jimbo Threpe meet his end? Le Zuan did not know. One could never anticipate the actions of an assassin, especially one as unpredictable as The Whip. Would the end that Manan wished for come in time? This game? Next game? Le Zuan downed his wine.

Let's see what happens…

***

Bullseye found herself screaming. "Move! Move!"

But Shadrack seemed groggy, drugged, sleepy, incapable of understanding her direction. Judwan strikers streaked by, and he couldn't seem to raise an arm to stop them. He was like an old, senile man who had wandered too far from home and didn't know which turn to make.

Finally, jack Jerold Minata came up and slapped him on the helmet. The slap at first angered the confused guard. He pushed Jerold away. They got into a small scuffle as the game continued around them. Bullseye's focused screaming finally moved the mountain.

Shadrack put out his arm and slammed a Mystic to the ground. Bullseye could hear the thin, pale Judwan's neck snap even from the sidelines. The slam brought a rare collective gasp from the Mystic fans who knew that their player was out of the game and perhaps dead. A medibot rolled onto the field and pulled the broken player away.

Bullseye hated playing against the Judwan. She hated playing against any alien team whose inherent racial attributes gave them—in her opinion—an unfair advantage on the pitch. Sure, the Judwan were fragile. They had proven that again today. Still, teams like them and the Terratons, with their ability to teleport, weren't fair. Over her career, she had been on the record complaining about it more than once. No one cared, neither the GCPS nor Digby. So, here they were, playing against a team that could, by simple motion alone, leave the Vipers looking like drooling babies in a crib. The Judwan didn't even need to wear gloves to catch the ball. Their long arms and fingers were naturally suited to capturing a sphere of titanium at one hundred fifty miles per hour.

Life sucked sometimes, as she had learned in her long, long career. Sometimes, Bullseye wished she were still on a battlefield somewhere, hiding in a pile of wrenched tank metal, waiting for a sweet target to fall into the reticle. Then... pop! Right between the eyes. A bullet in the forehead was always the best way to handle a problem, she knew. In DreadBall, unfortunately, there was no magic bullet.

Maddog King was playing well. He had not been the focal point of the Mystics' plan to beguile and confuse; Shadrack had taken the brunt of that strategy. So Maddog had been able to work with near impunity, racking up a goodly portion of slams and even one kill. They had acquired two kills now with Shadrack's most recent slam. Things were looking good. The Vipers were up by two, and the game was coming to a close.

Leeland was at her side, but he was focused on Jimbo's and Little Frankie's weak cognitive resistance to Judwan feints, which had confused the strikers once again and forced them to surrender the ball. A Judwan striker whom they called 'Pellet' now had a lane to the Viper back goal. The chase was on.

Jacks Me-Shan Lo and Jerold Minata back-pedaled to keep Pellet in front of them. Maddog and Shadrack pursued.

Maddog was not as large as Shadrack, but he was faster. He pushed aside a Mystic striker who tried his mind tricks on King and found himself without three sharp teeth in his upper plate. Maddog pushed another Mystic aside and leaped forward, splaying out like a cat making dough. He struck the pitch hard, but not before grazing his left glove against Pellet's Achilles heel.

The Mystic striker stumbled forward and held his arms out to keep his body from slamming into the pitch. Jimbo Threpe was there to rip the ball out of his long fingers.

The game suddenly shifted back into Viper control. Time was running out.

"Strike the goal!" Leeland shouted near Bullseye's ear. She pushed him away and kept her focus on her guards who were having trouble changing direction so suddenly and providing protection for their ball carrier.

The top of the stadium churned, and a shower of brilliant red and blue and yellow light colorized the pitch surface, making even Bullseye swoon. What pleasant, restful patterns they were, and she had to resist staring into them and falling asleep.

I hate the Judwan!

The kaleidoscopic patterns did not seem to bother Maddog, however, as he moved quickly to keep pace with Jimbo and provide muscle to the striker's last move to score. Some men were just immune to such things, Bullseye knew. Thankfully, Maddog seemed to be. Conner's suggestion of getting a Judwan priest into a practice session to work with their players was looking more appealing by the minute. Shadrack was having real problems with these puke green monks.

He had peeled off his pursuit and was again fumbling around as if he were suffering drug-addled apathy. "Come on, Shadrack," Bullseye screamed. "You're embarrassing me out there!"

But Shadrack was gone, done. He ripped off his helmet. His eyes rolled up into the back of his skull, and he dropped.

Jimbo ducked and dodged his way forward. Maddog had his back, Jerold had his right. Me-Shan had tried finding position to Jimbo's left, but he too was quite susceptible to Judwan suggestion. The rookie jack literally turned himself into the wall and slammed his head against the thick metal. A medibot rolled out to collect him.

Despite that horrible misfortune, Jimbo kept going. Maddog pushed aside a Mystic striker making one final attempt at stealing the ball. Jimbo paused in the two-score location of the strike zone, then moved three paces forward and gunned it home.

A perfect score. Time ran out, and the Vipers won it by three.

"That was most satisfying," Leeland said to Bullseye as they walked back to the visiting locker room. "Our first FSIDL victory."

"And not our last," Bullseye said, very much happy with her guards' performance, despite a few mishaps. "We should be able to prepare for our next opponent well enough. The Kushan Fangs are nothing but Veer-myn. They should be easy to—"

Bullseye turned abruptly to the cloaked figure who had struck her shoulder on pass by.

"My apologies, sir," she said, disoriented. "I didn't see you there."

The figure grunted and waved its long, clawed arm. It turned its hooded head toward her, and Bullseye caught a glimpse of the hideous face behind the grey fabric.

A Veer-myn, its long, rodent face peeking out from beneath the hood. Sweat and stink flowed from its porous skin, the part not covered with sticky brown fur anyway. Bullseye stared into the face, trying to meet the creature's eyes. But it had only one eye. The missing one was not covered with a patch. The eye was nothing more than a dry, empty, black hole, lined with red scars like a spider's web. Bullseye's stomach churned.

The Veer-myn smiled, waved her off, and walked away.

Bullseye shivered.

"Everything all right?" Leeland asked, the concern on his face sincere.

She shook her head, rubbed her face. "I'm fine, I'm fine. I thought I saw a ghost from my—it's nothing. It's just this stadium. I think it's getting to me like Shadrack."

"Well, let's get to our locker room and celebrate. That first win is the most important."

Indeed it was, Bullseye knew. She shook her head again, turned away from the creature who had disappeared into the leaving crowd, and followed Leeland to the locker room.

***

It was her! It was her! And she recognized me. She recognized me!

Cegrich Wick was so pleased, he didn't even care that he and his spotter had missed a perfect opportunity to put a slug into Jimbo's head. In truth, Cegrich had not even taken the safety off his rifle as he perched there in the girders of the Judwan stadium, hidden behind all the riotous colors cascading through the mirrors at the top of the dome. A perfect place to sit and wait for a chance to squeeze off a round. It did not matter now. All that mattered was *her*, Carla Bullseye Bock. She had felt fear when she had looked into his cavernous eye. He could see the fear, the uncertainty, there on her pleasant, soulful, human face. The face of a killer.

His spotter approached, and in the chaos of thousands of fans leaving the stadium, who would care about two cloaked Veer-myn speaking in whispers? "You did not fire," the stooped creature said, showing the proper deference to his master. "I gave you the proper coordinates. Why, my Whip, did you not fire?"

Cegrich shrugged. "I did not feel like it."

"But it was a perfect chance to—"

"I will decide when the time is perfect!"

The creature stooped low. "Yes, my Whip. I serve at your pleasure. Shall we now plan for the next game?"

Cegrich shook his head. The motion was like a dog stepping out of a pool of water as a shiver of joy, of excitement, ran down his sharp, bare spine. "Are you stupid? Assassinating a human striker in a Veer-myn stadium? I will not give the GCPS an excuse to condemn and kill more Veer-myn than they already do, every day. I accomplished what I came here to do. There will be another chance for Mackinaw Jim's head down the road. The season is long, and you will serve me well in time.

"Now, come," he said, grabbing his spotter's shoulder and turning him toward the direction he wished to go. "Let us find food. I've a man-sized appetite for something raw and bloody."

Oh, how he wished it could be Carla Bock's corpse that he dined on. But no. Not yet. Soon, though. Soon, he would have a chance to feast on her bones.

Cegrich Wick smiled as he walked out of the stadium and into the warm, white light of the sun. *Soon... very, very soon...*

Chapter 10

Leeland waved his hand over the security panel on the apartment door. Lights flashed, followed by a faint ring of a bell on the opposite side, and the door opened. His heart raced. He didn't know what to expect. *I shouldn't be here so late.*

But it had been arranged, quietly and without press fanfare, by Goethe. They were expecting him. He didn't know what to expect.

The door opened. A little girl greeted him.

Victoria. Leeland recognized her from the brief moment that she had appeared at the press conference. Short, thin, with black curly hair. She smiled. Leeland smiled back.

The door opened further. Victoria's mother stepped up.

"Come in," she said, humbly holding the door open to allow access. "Best to do it quickly, so the press doesn't see you."

Leeland obliged and walked in. "Thank you for seeing me. I apologize for the late hour, but I thought it best. Less snoops out at this time of night."

"Of course," she said.

He offered his hand. She took it reluctantly. "I'm sorry. I didn't catch your name at the press conference. You are..."

"Heather Brush," she said.

"Nice to meet you, Heather." Leeland then turned to Victoria, who had taken a seat on a nearby couch. "And you must be Victoria."

"Victoria Brush-Roth," the girl said. "My mom lets me have my daddy's name."

"Indeed," Leeland said. "And it's a good name."

"Sit down, please," Heather said, motioning to the couch. Leeland nodded and took a seat next to Victoria. She sidled up next to him with a warm smile as if they were old friends.

"You look like the pictures of my daddy," Victoria said. "I never met my dad for real. Just pictures. You look like him."

Leeland smiled. "Thank you. I always thought he was the best looking Roth in the family. You look like him too."

"Vicky," Heather said. "Will you go to your room for a little bit? I need to speak with your uncle alone."

Victoria seemed deflated. She blew a strand of hair out of her face and got up. She turned to Leeland, waved, and went off down the long hallway to the back of the apartment.

"Would you like something to drink?" Heather asked. "Coffee? Tea?"

Leeland waved her off. "No, thank you. I'm fine."

She leaned back into her chair, sighed. "Then let's get to it. Why are you here, Mr. Roth?"

"Call me Leeland," he said. "Or Leelee. My defensive coach calls me that, but I don't think she'd mind if—"

"I don't want your money."

Leeland shook his head. "I'm not offering you any."

"Then why are you *here*?"

Leeland paused before answering. He could see that Heather was angry. A totally understandable emotion for the moment, but he wanted to make sure that he answered in such a way as to not induce his own anger and frustration. It wasn't his fault that Victor was a lout, got this woman pregnant, then abandoned her. *Not my fault at all.*

"I wanted to meet my niece," he said, low and quiet, "and her mother. I thought, what with all the rumors and hearsay floating around, it would be best to get ahead of the situation and—"

"Oh, I see. This is just to cover your own butt and make sure Victor's indiscretions don't damage you and your stupid team."

Patience... patience, Leeland... "No, that isn't it at all. But I've spent most of my adult life in the spotlight, Ms. Brush, and I know that your press conference won't be the end of it. You've been able to protect your daughter from all of it so far, but how long do you think that will last? I guarantee the questions will continue, and eventually, they'll corner your daughter and ask her questions."

Heather shook her head. Leeland thought it would fall off. "I won't allow it. I'll kill them first."

Leeland smiled, admiring her spirit. "You may try. But already other rumors about Victor are coming to light. All a pile of Zee waste, I can tell you that, but nevertheless, they are out there. It's happening because someone is intent on destroying me, the Roth family name, Victor's name, and the Vitala Vipers. I have my suspicions as to who it is, but it isn't going to stop unless we get ahead of it and *make* it stop. We can't do that unless we, to borrow one of my defensive coach's military terms, 'join forces.'"

Heather glared at him. If her eyes were sharp, he'd have been cut a dozen times already. He could also see the exhaustion behind those sharp eyes, the kind of exhaustion that comes from clinging to a hope that you know is worth clinging to, but feeling angry because it keeps slipping away. Heather must have thought that holding that press conference would take the pressure off her and her daughter. But she had to know now that that was not going to happen. The wolves were at the door, and they would not stop clawing until they got to the little piggies inside.

"What are you proposing?" she asked.

Leeland rubbed his hot face, gathered his thoughts, and said, "First, I want to apologize for my brother's behavior. As much as I can do so, I apologize. My brother was many things, but I had no knowledge of you... or of any other women he might have done this to. We were on separate teams and lived separate lives for the most part. I truly had no knowledge.

"What I propose is that you and Victoria come live at the Viper Training Complex, if only for the rest of the season. There, I can guarantee that you and Victoria will not be hounded by the press."

"But you hold press conferences all the time," Heather said, throwing up her hands in exasperation. "I'm quite familiar with the sport, Leeland. I know how it works. How is the Viper training complex a better place?"

"It's a fortress, Heather. Yes, the press come and go all the time, but do you honestly think this apartment, as nice as it is, is a safer place to live? With the rumors out there now of Victor conspiring with Rebs, this is not a safe place to be." Leeland scooted up to the edge of the couch and leaned closer to Heather. "The universe is a dangerous place, Heather. Let me help you keep the wolves at bay."

He didn't mean to terrify the woman, but if it made her see the truth of the situation, so be it. Perhaps it would have been best to send Bullseye to convince her of the reality of the situation. Bullseye was an ex-corporate sniper. She understood the dangers out there in the Spheres more so than he did. And perhaps two women speaking about these matters would have been better. But Victor was his brother. It was Leeland's responsibility to try to make this right.

A tear ran down Heather's cheek. "You know," she said, wiping her face, "Victoria is right. You look like your brother. Just not as cute.

"I was a stupid college kid on break, enjoying the beaches of Alacarte with friends. Victor was there on vacation with some of the other players from the Jade Dragons. Oh, he was a marvelous specimen, your brother. Tall, muscular, with a full body bronze tan. A charmer too, respectful, funny. I fell for it all. One thing led to another, and we were hanging out all week, my friends and his friends. Things got serious two days into it... and here I am."

Her pleasant reminiscence got serious as her smile turned to a frown. "Three months later, I found out that I was pregnant. I tried contacting Victor to tell him. I was afraid of what he might say, but I was still wrapped up in the glow of our time together. I never expected him to ignore me.

"A week later, a bunch of lawyers and goons in suits show up at my parents' door, demanding to talk to me. Imagine how that felt, Leeland, men representing your brother hounding me to sign a document declaring that Victor was *not* the father? Five men in black suits. After two hours of intimidation, I signed it just to get them out of my face. Can you imagine how that felt?"

No, he could not, but he did not answer. From her expression, he could tell that any word from him at this moment would be met with sharp defiance. She was angry. She was hurt. She was exhausted. She just wanted all this to go away.

He waited a moment longer, then dared to speak. "Please, Heather, come to the complex. Let Kapoor Industries protect you. Let me protect you. Let me get to know my niece. You let Victoria use her father's surname. Give me an opportunity to show her a side of the Roth family that isn't associated with abandonment."

Heather stared at him through watery eyes, as if she were trying to decide if *this* Roth brother could be trusted.

Yes, yes, a thousand times, you can trust me, Leeland thought, but again, did not say. *And if I* don't *treat you right, Carla will kick my butt!*

Heather took a long time to answer. She got up, paced the room, cried some more, hugged herself, and rubbed her arms as if the room were cold. Finally, she sat back down, sighed, wiped her face clean, and said, "Okay, Victoria and I will come with you. But don't you be thinking I'm going to be your woman or anything. I've had enough of the Roths to last a lifetime."

Leeland smiled and put up his hand. "I assure you, this isn't about that at all."

Chapter 11

Their conversation took the better part of a full day, as their messages back and forth were transferred through a series of communication buoys positioned at key checkpoints throughout the spheres. Leeland would ask a question—several questions, in fact—and Aryan would answer them. Follow-ups to those answers were inevitably required, and on and on it went. Leeland spent the lag time doing menial team paperwork.

Security authorizations, uniform and equipment checks. A medical review with the team physicians to discuss the myriad cuts and bruises and sores and sprains: who had them and what was being done about them. Signatures to approve the list of food and souvenir vendors attending the first home game. Reviewing the final touches on their stadium, concerns about this or that not being ready when the Nemion Oceanics 'swam' into town. And scores of other matters that the owner of the team could (and should) be doing. Many of the matters could be resolved by Aryan even through the myriad light years that separated them. Electronic signatures could be acquired for sure. But why bother? Leeland was more than capable of doing these simple tasks, and since he was there, in the midst of it all, it made sense for him to simply serve in Aryan's stead. For now, anyway.

The latest batch of answers came through. Leeland sat at his desk and reviewed them.

"There are no indications that the rumors are being generated from Vitala or anywhere else in the Third Sphere," Aryan said, his voice distant and hollow, *"but I do agree*

with you that Saanvi is probably behind it. The Kaala Pani prison allows its inmates to communicate on a limited basis with outside entities. Conversations are reviewed, of course, but someone like my sister would have a way around those checks. The only way we'll know for sure is to go and visit her. And that's what I'll do before heading to Hope.

"And yes, you have my expressed permission to serve in my stead until I arrive. Your signature is as good as mine. If anyone gives you grief about that, you point them to me. Don't worry, Leeland, I'll take the tedium off your shoulders soon enough. And finally, yes, I would like the couch to stay in my office."

Leeland had already been putting his signature on documents, but now he had verbal authorization to back it up. Very well. The visit to Saanvi was what concerned him the most in Aryan's answers.

Leeland activated his comm and replied, "Okay, all that is fine, save for your proposed visit to Saanvi. Aryan, I'm not happy about that. You know how she is. She'll get her claws into you and... well, it's a risk. If you go, make sure you take a battery of lawyers with you and, hell, some muscle as well. She's probably paid off the guards. Be careful."

He tapped his tablet and sent the reply. He leaned back into his chair for a breather. Shapshir Goethe stepped into his office.

"Good afternoon, Boss," the liaison said. "Sorry to disturb your nap."

Leeland sat up straight and rubbed his face. "I wish you *were* interrupting a nap. I wish I had the time to take one."

Shapshir nodded. "I understand. This won't take long. I've only got two items that need your attention."

"Shoot."

"First, the SportsBlast Food and Drug Corporation would like the Vitala Vipers to participate in an advertisement campaign, along with a few other teams in the FSIDL. They want to showcase their latest flavor of DreadMax high-energy drink by using members of the newest teams in the league, along with some serious up-and-coming rookies."

Leeland wrinkled his brow. "What?"

"Yes. They'd like to start filming as soon as possible." Shapshir furrowed his brow as well, and his voice seemed to match Leeland's frustration.

Leeland sighed loud enough to make Shapshir cringe as the Asterian put his hands on his hips and shook his head at the ground. *As if we have time for such nonsense!* Advertising was standard practice in DreadBall, Leeland knew. When he was a member of the Trontek 29ers, advertisers were always hounding him for screen time, and he had obliged more than once. It was a way to get exposure, especially for those so-called 'up-and-comers.' It was a way to shed positive light on the team, and it was a way to make serious endorsement megacredits, even more than by playing the game. But who had the time for such nonsense now? Certainly not him, and certainly not the team.

Leeland sighed again, relenting. "Fine. But I'm not raising a finger to coordinate any of this. You take charge of it or get someone else to do it. You just tell me when and where to show up, and we'll show up."

Shapshir nodded. "No problem, Boss. It'll be handled."

"Good. Now, you said you had two things to discuss?"

"Yes." Shapshir paused, then said, "Heather Brush and her daughter Victoria are here."

Leeland shot out of his seat. "Blazing stars, Shapshir," racing to the door, "why didn't you tell me this first?"

The Asterian liaison couldn't contain his mirth. "Because if I had, we'd have never discussed the advertisement."

***

"We've given you one of the MVP rooms," Leeland said, showing Heather and Victoria to their quarters. "I apologize that it isn't very roomy; its purpose, really, is to accommodate one player for one week. But it's the best accommodations we have, given that this building was—"

Heather raised her hand. "It's fine, Leeland. No worries."

Leeland waited patiently as Heather and Victoria began unpacking their belongings. They had only a few bags filled with clothing for the most part, a few pictures in small frames, some plushies, and a few basic toiletries. Leeland was about to tell them that they did not require such items, as the adjoining bathroom had all of those things for them. But these people weren't his players, and he was neither their coach nor their boss. He had invited them here to live in peace and in whatever way they wanted.

"The, ah, press didn't give you any trouble upon your arrival, did they?"

Heather shook her head. "No, although they know we are here. It has already been reported." She pulled a few blouses from her bag and hung them up in a closet that slid open on the wall. She placed a couple pairs of shoes there as well. "But your idea of us arriving whenever we wanted seems to have kept them guessing as to when and where we would arrive. There weren't many guarding the back gate to the loading dock."

Leeland nodded. "You have my liaison, Shapshir Goethe, to thank for much of that. He's had the press scrambling all week, tracking useless little stories and rumors and what have you. I'm beginning to think he's a Chovar Psychic."

It was an efficiency apartment. The entire living space was wide open, save for the bathroom and shower compartment. Leeland had ordered an additional bed delivered. It sat next to the space occupied by the main bed that slid in and out of the wall upon verbal request. When both beds were fully deployed, it left little space in the bedroom.

Victoria didn't seem to care, however. She had ordered the main bed deployed and was now jumping from one to the other as she hugged tightly some kind of plushy.

"Be careful, Vicky," her mother said. "Don't break those beds."

Leeland waved off her concern. "Don't worry about that. Those beds are made for DreadBall-sized bodies."

He watched Victoria play for a little while then, resisting the urge to check the time, said, "Well, I will leave you both to it. Thank you for agreeing to come here. I'm sure everything will work out." He pointed to the wall. "When you are settled in, contact me via that panel and we'll have dinner, and then I'll give you a tour of the place. Most of the facility is empty, but—"

"Why don't you take Victoria with you now?" Heather said, pausing her unpacking to accentuate her comment with a strong, positive expression. "It'll give her something to focus her energy on and give you both a little time to get acquainted."

Victoria jumped to the floor, stumbled a little, but recovered and made her way to Leeland. "Can we see the stadium first?" she asked.

Leeland nodded, then looked at Heather for confirmation. "If you don't mind..."

Heather shook her head. "No, show her everything. Get her nice and tired and hungry for dinner. I'll meet you there with Carla."

Leeland pulled his head back in surprise. "Carla?"

"Yes. She asked that I let her know I was here."

Leeland had a million questions about that. Had they spoken already? Had they already met? Why would Bullseye want to speak with her? A million questions, but he asked none of them.

He figured he wouldn't like the answers.

***

Leeland took Victoria to the stadium. He flicked on the lights and let her walk from back goal to back goal. He even let her heft one of the now still and silent titanium balls. Everything in the stadium, every seat, every goal, every inch, was brand new. Leeland couldn't help but feel a tingle down his spine. Soon, the space would be a cacophony of shouting fans, boisterous color-commentators, and DreadBall players knocking the Zee out of one another. It would lose its pristine state quickly. But for today, it was a child's playground, and Victoria moved from goal to goal, pretending to score and respond to the accolades of adoring fans.

"You were a player too, right?" Victoria asked him. "When my daddy was alive?"

"Oh, yes," Leeland said, accepting the ball from her small hands. For show, he raised it up, held it for a minute, then tossed it as hard as he could across the pitch. It struck the floor below the opposing back goal and rolled to the wall. The injuries he had suffered in the tournament championship game had healed, but it had been quite a while since he had made a throw. And the last time he had thrown an inactive ball, well, he couldn't remember. His shoulder ached from the strain of the toss. "I'm quite out of shape these days. But your father and I played many a DreadBall match. He was one of the best. I was proud to be his brother."

Does she know that I killed her father? Certainly, she must. How could she not? Even if her mother had shielded her from the truth of it, she must have heard something about it by now in the press. Victoria was a smart child, and very alert. She knew, and Leeland wondered if the expression on her face right now revealed the truth of that knowledge. Did she want to say something about it? It was hard to know.

They visited the Vitala training room next, where some of the Vipers were working out. "Clean up your language, boys," Leeland shouted as they entered. "We've a lady in the house."

Victoria greeted each of them in turn: Little Frankie, Spencer, Dillon, Lucas, and Me-Shan Lo.

"Where is everyone else?" She asked.

"We're working in shifts today, young lady," Frankie said. "Get too many of us in such a small space, we never get anything done."

"And you need the practice," Lucas said with a wink.

Frankie pushed him away. "Go bake your head."

"Where's Jimbo Threpe?" Victoria asked. "He's the one I want to meet."

They all laughed at that, including Frankie who then pretended to be disappointed. "I'll have you know, I'm ten times better than that chump. You just watch me in the next game."

Leeland put his hands on Victoria's shoulders. "Come on... let's move on and let these vagabonds earn their keep."

They waved goodbye, and Leeland shuffled Victoria out the door.

"They seem like nice men," she said as they rode the elevator up to the second floor.

"They are," he replied. "A little rough around the edges, but they'll do for a DreadBall team."

He showed her all of their offices and even the media center, though there were no press conferences scheduled today, and the room was dark and quiet. As they moved from place to place, Leeland tried explaining to her as much as he could about the game and business of DreadBall. He tried keeping it simple and straightforward, not confusing his information with complex and tedious details that would probably fly over Victoria's head. For her part, she seemed intrigued by everything he said, and Leeland wondered if she were trying to figure out where her father had fit into all of it. She knew that he was a striker, for sure, but what exactly did that mean? Some of these details he simply couldn't convey to her in an afternoon tour of the facility. Those details would come to her as she attended and watched games. Assuming her mother allowed her to, of course.

When they got to his office, Leeland saw the red light flashing on his tablet, indicating Aryan's response to his latest comments. "Let's stay here for a moment, Victoria," he said, taking his seat and accepting the message. "Take a look around. There's a panel on the wall over there where you can access music or some cartoons."

"When are we going to meet Mama for dinner?" she asked.

"Right after I check my messages."

Aryan's response was somewhat hostile. Leeland turned down the sound so Victoria couldn't hear it from across the room.

"Look, Leeland, with all due respect, give me some credit. I'm not the same guy you met in that locker room

a year ago. I can handle my sister. She's in prison, for Zee's sake. If she is the source of these rumors about Victor, I must confront her. Don't worry. I'll be just fine. You do your job, and I'll do mine."

"Why is he so angry?"

Leeland jumped at Victoria's voice. He had been so wrapped up in Aryan's response he had not realized that she had sidled up next to him.

He turned his tablet off. "Ah, he's just contrary no matter what. It's fine."

"He said my daddy's name," she said. "Is he trying to find out if the rumors about my father are true?"

Leeland didn't know what to say. Best to keep Victoria totally out of any of this, but it was his fault that she had seen and heard the conversation. He could have simply waited until later, after dinner, when she and Heather were back in their room. *Stupid, stupid!*

"Yes, he is," Leeland said, rising from his chair and offering Victoria his hand. "He'll take care of everything. I promise. Come, let's go eat!"

Victoria took his hand, and they took the elevator down to the first floor and the cafeteria.

Many of the players who had not been in the training room were there. Leeland introduced them all, including Jimbo Threpe, whom Victoria went right up to and hugged. "You're the best!" she said.

Jimbo couldn't agree more.

They sat down at the table with Heather and Bullseye—with the latter wearing the largest grin he had ever seen. And were those canary feathers sticking out of her mouth? She had the kind of sheepish expression that suggested she had just swallowed one.

"What are you grinning at?" Leeland asked as Victoria began telling her mother about their tour.

"Oh, nothing, nothing," Bullseye said, taking a sip of tea and winking.

"And what did you guys talk about while we were away?"

"Just stuff," she said, maintaining that grin. "Nothing you need to worry about."

Leeland buried his face into the menu of the day, saying nothing to that, but knowing that when Bullseye Bock told you not to worry, that was the time to worry the most.

Chapter 12

The Kushan Fangs' Stadium

The Fangs used an old bio-dome as their stadium. It was a relic from the early expansion of the GCPS. Now, having fallen into disrepair, with its dome cracked and even breached in places, its pitch was a latticework of muddy puddles, moss, cracks, and other detritus that had blown in through the gaps or had been strewn about by the fans. But what mattered—the goals, the ball cannon, the strike zones—worked perfectly. The Kushan Fangs took their DreadBall seriously, and they took no time making that clear.

They snatched the ball on the first rush, using their guards to clear a path to the closest Viper goal. Leeland knew that the Fangs believed in the Veer-myn philosophy of 'strike first, strike often.' A team comprised primarily of strikers, with an occasional line-up of two guards, couldn't afford to waste time trading slams. The Fang striker who nabbed the whistling titanium sphere dodged Shadrack Menapi and Lucas Buck and punched the ball into the closest goal.

The Fangs were up by one and on the move again.

A striker named Binji 'The Squeak' caught the ball on the second launch. This time, however, he tried for a deep score.

Conner was coaching from the sidelines again, and he barked orders to jacks Lucas and Artemis. "Fall back! Shadow the ball carrier!"

Leeland had decided not to castle (surprise, surprise!) and so the back goal was wide open and waiting to be fed. Lucas and Artemis pedaled back on Conner's orders. Binji tried twice to stop and make a two-point score, but the Vipers defense was holding well after their shock of being scored on first. They were running with a 2-2-2 lineup, a nice, balanced attack that seemed to now be giving the Fangs some trouble.

Then a Veer-myn guard slipped past Shadrack, put out its long arm, and raked Lucas' shoulder with razor-sharp claws. Lucas stumbled three feet to his left, and that was just enough to open a lane to the back goal for Binji to score. He slid into a three-point position and gunned it home.

Suddenly, the Fangs were up by four, and panic flashed on every Viper face. The Kushan fans wailed their joy and beat their feet upon the makeshift wood and iron bleachers surrounding the pitch, such that glass from the dilapidated bio-dome shook loose and fell atop the referee.

Play proceeded despite the ref getting hammered by glass. Leeland was about to bark out an order to Artemis when two Gaelians and one Rin invaded the pitch, running madly around the scoring zones and waving pro-Reb flags. The fans, shocked and disoriented at first, began to boo and hiss. A couple Fang players tried knocking down the Rebel sympathizers, but the Gaelians were fairly large. Security bots swarmed in.

"Time is called momentarily!" said the voice from the Eye in the Sky.

Leeland felt a shiver run down his spine as he recalled the horrific Reb attack during the Vipers' tournament run in the Third Sphere. A lot of good people had been killed during that attack, including Viper star guard 'Backhoe' Bertuchi, who had sacrificed himself to bring the devastation to an end. What a terrible, terrible moment. But Leeland shook the memory from his mind and took advantage of the pause.

"Okay," he said, his starting lineup gathered round, "we go into castle. Shadrack, Caesar, you guard the back goal.

Down by four, we're not letting them score a sudden victory on one shot." He looked at Jimbo Threpe. "You need to do something you don't like to do, but you must. Forget scoring. We'll use Frankie for that and bring in Kirkus if necessary. I want you to use your legendary throwing skills to brain The Squeak."

Just saying it brought up bad memories again in Leeland's mind. Heather and Vicky would be watching the game from the Viper complex. What would they think seeing Leeland order the very foul that he had used against Victor? He shook the thought from his mind. No time for doubt now. They couldn't afford going down by two games so early in the season.

Leeland slapped Jimbo on the helmet. "Did you hear me?"

Jimbo nodded. "I heard you, Boss. I've never killed a DreadBall player before."

"Who said anything about killing him? You just need to knock him out of the game."

"Yeah, but you know better than anyone how these things can go."

The silence of the other players was palpable, even within the deafening cacophony of the Kushan fans and the security bots subduing the Reb sympathizers. Leeland stared his star striker down. "I'm well aware of the potential outcome, Jimbo. Don't you worry about me. You just do your duty for the team. Understood?"

The strategy session was over. The Reb sympathizers had been subdued and removed. A new referee that wasn't impaled with a dozen shards of bio-dome glass was put into play, and the ball was fired down the center line.

Little Frankie scooped it up and moved to score.

A Kushan striker who tried to pick his pocket went down from a massive slam from Artemis. A few clever moves later and Frankie took a two-point shot that brought the Fang lead down to two.

Leeland breathed a sigh of relief. A two-point game was quite manageable, so long as he could keep it that way long enough to give his team a chance for a late-game win. Doing so would require maintaining the castle.

The ball was fired back into play. Jimbo snatched it right up.

Leeland was now having second thoughts about his order to Jimbo. Artemis and Lucas had dropped a couple strikers, and so the Fangs had more benchwarmers on the pitch as their starting lineup began absorbing injuries. A one-point goal was quite easy for Jimbo to make right now. But Leeland did not shout new orders to his striker, as Jimbo dodged a Fang guard to get into position to fire a line drive straight into The Squeak's chest.

Leeland had never seen a ball fired so quickly and so perfectly: a straight line shot rocketing off Jimbo's electromagnetic scoop in a blur of silver and blue. It struck The Squeak in the back, right between the shoulder blades, and sent him into the wall.

Red warning lights flashed, and the Eye in the Sky boomed. *"Jimbo Threpe! You have committed a foul. You are out of the game. Leave immediately!"*

Two medibots swooped in and carried Binji's limp body away. Jimbo left the pitch. The game continued.

The action swayed back and forth with the Fangs holding their modest two-point lead. Leeland then made a fateful decision.

He waved to Shadrack. "Break the castle. Go cruising."

Both Shadrack and Caesar moved out of castle and began knocking heads. The momentum shifted, and the ball fell into Kirkus Tetsudo's glove.

Lucas and Artemis cleared his path, and Kirkus quickly moved into the two-point position of the nearest goal, fired the ball, and scored.

The score fell to zero, the ball was launched on the center line, and the final rush began.

Neither team claimed the ball at first. It ricocheted out of a puddle, skipped off a large crack on the pitch, and struck Lucas Buck in the head, knocking him down, but otherwise, causing no harm. Two Veer-myn and Artemis Hale went after it.

Hale got there first, scooping the ball out of the water and moving to score. It seemed at first that he didn't know what to do with the ball, as if he was confusing his position as jack with a guard. He moved to keep out of the reach of a Fang guard and overlooked easy opportunities to try a score. Then it seemed to Leeland that his jack finally understood: the score was at zero and all they needed was one shot on goal.

Artemis ducked a swipe from the Fang guard and slid into the closest strike zone. "Take the shot!" both Leeland and Conner shouted across the pitch. If it failed, the game would go into overtime. No harm, no foul. "Take the shot!"

Artemis moved forward a step to set himself up for a one-point shot. He raised his glove and angled his arm to throw, and then took a slam from his blind spot by a Fang guard that lifted him into the air, slammed him down, and rode him across the pitch as his armor broke apart.

The ball popped from Artemis' glove, but Little Frankie was there to snatch it before it hit the ground. He slid into the strike zone and slammed the ball home.

Time ran out, and the Vipers took the game by one.

The crowd fell silent as Leeland and Conner and the rest of the Viper team celebrated. Then Leeland heard the medibot call 'code black, code black' and his heart skipped a beat.

The Vipers had won the game, but Artemis Hale was dead.

Kaala Pani Prison, Third Sphere Industrial World Vitala, Zaigor System

Despite his push-back against Leeland's skepticism, Aryan truly had no desire to be here, facing his sister. She looked the same, save for the purple jumpsuit. Her dark hair was longer now, and Aryan couldn't help but admire her beauty and her stoic visage as she was ushered into the visitor's lounge in wrist and ankle restraints. She was his sister, after all, and a Kapoor. Even in prison, a member of the family should carry themselves with dignity and grace.

The guards sat her down across from him. The reinforced ferro-glass in between caught the glare of the overhead lights, reflecting a blurry image of her on the glass, making her seem larger, more ominous.

Aryan leaned back in his chair. "Hello, Saanvi."

She paused, blinked several times, then let a smile slip across her lips. "Hello, little brother. Good of you to pay a visit before running off to your plaything. Congratulations are in order, yes? Two wins, one loss. Not a bad start for a back-alley team like the Vipers."

Aryan nodded, ignoring her attempt at getting a rise. "Leeland knows what he's doing."

"Yes. He may be the only one on the team that does. Do you know... I told him once that he always had a place in

Kapoor Industries. A lie, of course, but perhaps he should have taken a position. Perhaps he would have run the company better than current management."

Aryan shook his head. "He's where he needs to be... as are others."

Saanvi moved closer to the glass. Aryan knew her expression, the one she always wore before blowing up. Like a tiger assessing her prey, ready to pounce. "I guess that means me, eh? I'm right where I need to be?"

Aryan shrugged and adjusted his sitting position. "Hey, you do the crime you must do—"

She waved him off. "Spare me your foolish, adolescent expressions, little brother, and tell me why you are here."

Indeed, it was time to get to it. Aryan looked at the minutes remaining displayed on the ferro-glass.

"Very well," he said. "A woman who knows the Viper record must also know of the terrible—and *false*—rumors of Victor Roth's involvement with Rebels."

"False?" Saanvi's voice leapt into a higher register. "How can you be so sure? The 'rumors' of the ladies he abandoned with children were true."

Aryan nodded. "There is a wide gap between personal misconduct and acts of sedition, Saanvi, which you should know all about."

"As should you," she said, admirably holding her anger in check. "If there was justice in the GCPS, you'd be on this side of the glass, and I on the other."

"What do you know of these *charges*?"

"Nothing!" She barked, falling back into her chair such that it cracked slightly. A guard moved to assist. Saanvi waved him off.

Aryan chuckled. "Impressive, big sister. You've got them trained already."

"Watch it, Aryan," Saanvi said, her expression turning from frustration to clear anger. Aryan was glad the glass had been reinforced. "These walls aren't so thick as to protect you."

"Ah, so you are involved. You can reach out beyond the bars."

Saanvi shook her head. "I speak only to family, Aryan. Family only. That is all that is left for me in here and all that I wish to care about." She breathed deeply, calming herself. "Who Victor Roth was or was not involved with is no concern of mine."

"Nor mine. I could care less about Victor. But this isn't about him. This is about Leeland and the Vitala Vipers. A team, by the way, that exists because of you. You were the one who recommended it to father, not me."

"The only mistake I made in this whole mess."

Aryan nodded. "Perhaps, but here we are. The Kapoor name, our name, is now tied to the team's reputation. To Leeland's reputation. If they suffer under false rumors, the family name suffers. Do you want the family to suffer?"

Saanvi grew deathly silent. Aryan watched as time ticked away. Finally, with a minute left, she said, "Go, little brother. Go chase after your snakes." She motioned to the guard. "We're done here."

Aryan stood. "Stop the rumors, Saanvi. If you are the source of these rumors, I beg you, stop them... now!"

She stood as the guard grabbed her arm. "Nice talking to you, Aryan. Give Leeland a big, wet kiss for me." She winked and giggled as they took her away.

Aryan lingered a moment in silence, collecting his thoughts. He felt like crying. Not so much because of the slanderous accusations floating about, but for the lost time with Saanvi. There *was* a time when they were happy together, as children, when they would play and laugh and enjoy each other's company. Those were good times. Family times.

Family... that is all that is left for me in here...

Saanvi's words annoyed his thoughts, but they made sense. She could not leave Kaala Pani, so who could do the dirty work for her? A member of the family, of course.

Aryan waved to the guards to be let out, and as he walked away, one name came to mind. The only member of the family low enough, despicable enough, to work against the Kapoor name, against his own kin.

Manan...

Chapter 13

Viper Arena and Training Complex

"The Squeak will live," Conner said as he and Bullseye and Leeland met to discuss business before the Vipers' first home game against the Nemion Oceanics. "Though I hear he's out for the season, perhaps forever. Broken back. Fixable, of course, but he'll never be the same." He sighed. "Jimbo's pretty upset about it."

Leeland shook his head derisively. "He's such a prima. He acts like he's never played a single game in his life."

"He's a striker, Leelee," Bullseye said. "You of all people know how that is. Jimbo's never raised his hand to harm anyone."

"Yeah, well," Leeland said, "we gotta do what we gotta do. It was an important game to win."

"I agree," she said, shooting a careful glance in Conner's direction, "but such a blatant, open-air foul sends the message to future opponents that Mackinaw Jim is fair game. There'll be a target on his back for sure."

"Perhaps," Conner said, nodding, "it would have been best to give that order to a jack."

Leeland shook his head. "And The Squeak would have laughed it off. No. The only Viper capable of delivering the kind of shot needed was Jimbo. Whether he wishes to admit it or not, he knows it. He's just going to have to buck up and deal with it."

It was clear to Leeland that neither Bullseye nor Conner was happy with what had happened. Their dissatisfaction was not due to any affection or concern for The Squeak; they understood that in the course of play, casualties mounted. Their concern, he was certain, was about Jimbo and his current emotional state. Would their star striker be able to suit up and play to the level needed against a Sphyr team that, by all accounts, was one of the best in the FSIDL?

Leeland changed the subject with a question to Conner. "Have you decided on a replacement for Artemis?"

Conner nodded and sent Leeland the list from his tablet. "I have a few possibilities, but the decision won't solidify until after our match against the Oceanics. We'll be going into that game a little understrength."

Leeland swiped through the list. All decent replacements, but no one stellar. Workmen-like options. Perhaps it was time to consider bringing in another MVP. But he shelved that discussion, and said, "I'm sure we'll be fine. You take care of this."

They discussed a few other matters, things that should be handled by Aryan, such as maintenance issues with the facility, personnel issues in the kitchen, budgetary concerns, and away-game travel expenses. Leeland finalized that conversation by silencing his tablet and leaning back in his chair for a closed-eye breather. Aryan was on his way, Leeland knew. He had had a conversation with him just that morning. His meeting with Saanvi had not gone well, as predicted, but Aryan did say that he was following up on some leads. What leads were those? Leeland wondered.

As he brought the meeting to a close, Shapshir Goethe burst into the room. "Ah, Mr. Goethe," Leeland said, standing, "I'm glad you've dropped by. I need you to—" The expression on the Asterian's face lacked its normal pleasantness, and Leeland did not finish his request. "What's wrong?"

Shapshir paused, looked at Bullseye and Conner, then said, "I'm sorry, Leeland, but the GCPS and Digby have both opened investigations."

Leeland shrugged. "That was to be expected. But they'll find nothing in Victor's background to suggest that he—"

"They'll be investigating him, yes," Shapshir said, "but it's you, Leeland. They're opening investigations on you."

"Total bull!" Bullseye's outburst was followed by her shoes pounding the hard floor. "Where do they have the right, and for what reason?"

The Asterian liaison cowered under Bullseye's glare. "They... certainly have the right, Bullseye, as much as we do not like it. As for reasons, well—"

"Their reasoning, obviously," Leeland interrupted, "is because of Saanvi's and Aryan's past relations with Rebs. Aryan's connections were juvenile and misguided, but otherwise, innocent. Saanvi's was sedition." Leeland huffed. "I'm in the center of my brother's accusations on one side and Kapoor Industries on the other." He sighed. "I guess I should have seen it coming."

"We'll fight it!" Bullseye said, and Leeland nodded agreement, but in his mind, his heart, he said, *I don't have the strength to do that. Just let it play out as it may.*

"Can't the FSIDL intervene on Leeland's behalf?" Conner asked.

Shapshir nodded. "Yes, in fact, their lawyers would like to talk with you soon, Leeland, to discuss legal options. Can I tell them you will meet with them this evening?"

"You can tell them anything you like," Leeland said, grabbing his tablet and walking to the door. "I have a meeting with *my* strikers right now."

"The press wants a word too," Shapshir said, this time in a much lower, quiet tone. "It has been a while since we've had a press conference and—"

Leeland turned on him, and even Bullseye and Conner cowered and stepped back a few paces. Leeland's face turned beet red; his jaw muscles pulsed like a jackhammer. "Mr. Goethe, you tell the press that if they wish to speak to Coach Leeland Roth about our upcoming game against the Nemion Oceanics, I'm happy to oblige. But if they want to talk about the ridiculous, and false, accusations about me and rebel contacts, you tell them that I'll personally kick their little Zee behinds out the door. You tell them that."

Bullseye called after him. Leeland ignored her and took the elevator to the first floor.

He took a step out of the elevator, his face burning, his mind a-swirl with a million tedious details, his anger hardly in check. To the right awaited his strikers. To the left and somewhere out there in Rosaria was a bar, a tavern, where perhaps all the answers to his problems lay. He took a step left, and then another, and another. He paused, sweat now beading on his forehead, his body shaking with the desire for just one drink, just one innocent little drink. Surely, that would be okay. Surely, just one little—

You look like the pictures of my daddy...

Victoria's words repeated in his mind, and Leeland paused.

How long he stood there, listening to her voice, he could not say. Viper and facility staff members passed by. He did not bother to acknowledge their presence. He simply stood there, staring left, remembering his years playing Xtreme DreadBall, the incalculable times that he had awakened in the Fourth Sphere with a bottle in his hand, a different woman at his side. All the sounds of his inevitable march to ruin, both positive and negative, cycling through his mind, over and over. But not a single sound was as pleasant and as meaningful as the girl's sweet voice.

Leeland shook his head and refocused on the world around him. Then, he turned, took a deep breath, and walked toward his strikers.

***

Good evening, and welcome to the first home game for the Vitala Vipers. Tonight's action is brought to you by MegaTech Sports, a division of the SportsBlast Food and Drug Corporation. I'm your host and color-commentator Josh Burkett. Listen to that crowd!

Well, yes, it is a bit muted, isn't it? That's because Hope and, in particular, our grand city of Rosaria, have yet to fully accept this plucky little Third Sphere team as their own. There are even those who want the Vipers to change their name to the Hope Diamonds or to the Rosaria Ragers. Petitions to make that happen are being signed as we speak, but tonight... tonight, the Vitala Vipers *will play under their Third Sphere name, and who will they be facing?*

The Nemion Oceanics are a very good team, indeed, and one that head coach Leeland Roth should not take for granted. Two arms, two legs, and one extremely powerful tail that not only provides protection from annoying strikers trying to steal the ball, but is in itself a good weapon to wield in the slam fest that I'm sure will dominate this game. The Sphyr hail from an ocean planet; they play wet, so it'll be interesting to see if Roth and his Vipers can keep a tight grip on anything, especially the ball.

Now, let's get to it. The cannon is loaded and ready to fire. Three...two...one...

***

The klaxons sounded, red and gold lights flashed throughout the Viper arena, and the ball was launched.

An Oceanic jack tried catching it on a leap, but Spencer Mills snagged it first. A splash of brackish water off the Sphyr's bluish-grey skin spattered his helmet's visor, but that didn't seem to deter the Viper striker's desire to reach the nearest strike zone and take a shot on goal. He twisted in place to avoid the jack's attempt at knocking the ball out of his glove with its meaty tail.

Leeland watched from the sidelines, shouting orders. "Keep it tight! Don't let them get behind you!" Chasing a Sphyr down the pitch was the least desirable thing to do in a game. Their tails not only served as a kind of rudder to maintain balance, but it made getting close nearly impossible. The key was to always be in their face.

With a few calculated bobs and weaves, Spencer reached the strike zone and tried to score. An Oceanic guard in his peripheral forced him to take the shot off-center. It struck the goal and bounced away. A mad scramble for the red-glowing titanium sphere ensued.

Leeland had always found it hard to describe a Sphyr. A kind of humanoid hammerhead shark with a cranial structure that looked as if it had been cleaved in two by an axe. Being an aquatic race meant that special showers had to be erected on their side of the pitch so that they could get a quick dousing as needed. The residual water itself was of little concern during play, except when there was a large mangle of bodies fighting for the ball.

Shadrack was sitting this one out due to a few leg injuries, so Maddog and Dillon Koch were trading fists with Oceanic guards trying to sweep their legs. Strikers on both teams were fighting for the ball. Somewhere in the pile were Little Frankie and Me-Shan Lo. Spencer was trying to reach the brawl but was struck from behind by the Oceanic jack who had drawn his number on ball launch. Spencer dropped hard and did not move.

A medibot flew onto the pitch to collect the woozy striker, and Leeland shouted, "Jerold, you're up!"

Jack Jerold Minata raced onto the pitch but held back from the ball pile and, instead, took a defensive position near the Vipers' three-point goal. No castling in this game, Leeland had ordered, no matter how badly it was going. He could take that chance against a team like the Oceanics. Sphyrs were tough, but not overly fast.

"You can put me in at any time, Boss," Jimbo said at Leeland's side. "I'm fine and ready to go."

Leeland nodded, but that wasn't the plan, unless things got desperate later in the game.

The ball popped out of the pile and struck Dillon on the helmet. Luckily, its speed had been diminished from the mad scramble, and thus, it merely knocked him down. He stood quickly, only to then be slammed by an Oceanic guard named Fahali. The press affectionately called the aquatic brute 'Fat Coral.' He was certainly one of the biggest Sphyr guards Leeland had ever seen. Dillon Koch's much smaller body should have been knocked across the pitch. But Dillon, perhaps needing to prove himself to an uninspired press corps that had begun questioning the small man's lackluster performances, ducked and took Fat Coral in the legs, lifted him up, and slammed him to the pitch.

Another medibot flew into the fray.

An Oceanic striker finally scooped up the ball, and the chase was on.

Jerold Minata now moved to intercept the Oceanic striker whose swishing tail was keeping Little Frankie at bay. Me-Shan Lo tried picking the pocket from the opposite side, only to be forced off target by an interfering Oceanic striker who put his wet face and cleaved head in Me-Shan Lo's line of sight. Jerold was now the only Viper in position to stop the score.

He shuffled to the left in an attempt to shadow the moves of the Oceanic striker. Leeland could see that Jerold found it difficult; the Sphyr striker was quite agile. But Jerold was no rookie. He knew that if he moved too close to the striker, then its quickness could be an impediment. He held back, seemingly a little too far, but Leeland could see the wisdom in his jack's decision.

The Oceanic striker interpreted Jerold's hesitancy to move closer as indecision. He stepped into the closest strike zone to try a two-point shot.

Jerold waited until the striker had committed to the throw. Then, he leapt, right into the path of the ball as it spiraled toward the goal at a smooth one hundred sixty miles per hour.

Jerold took the shot in the chest and fell right in front of the goal, unconscious and with perhaps a couple broken ribs. A medibot flew onto the pitch, and the ball was free again.

***

Finally, the crowd awakens! That was quite an impressive stop by Viper jack Jerold Minata. He may be out for the game, but he earned his pay tonight. Looks like we're in for what the ancients called a 'pitcher's duel.' I have no idea what that means, but there you are. Question now, is, who will Coach Roth send in to replace his unconscious jack?

***

"Send me in," Jimbo again implored at Leeland's side.

Leeland shook his head. "You'll go in when it's time to put you in. This is going to be a low-scoring affair. We have a full striker corps on the pitch, Jimbo. Let them play a while. You're not the only one who can score a goal."

Jimbo cursed and stalked away. Bullseye came up and whispered, "Why not put him in? He's ready, and the Oceanics look a little flat. If we score now, we can surely hold off till the end."

"You telling me how to coach now?"

The bite in the question took Bullseye by surprise. She stared at Leeland. A defiant twitch rippled across her bottom lip. "No, but I will if you don't get your mind out of whatever trouble it's drowning under."

Leeland turned to face her. "Oh, you can read minds now?"

She grabbed his arm. "I know exactly what you're thinking. You're letting all of these bogus rumors and investigations about your brother get to you. I understand how you feel, but now is not the time, Leeland. And you shouldn't take it out on Jimbo."

"Hey, he has a problem with the brutal realities of the game? He wants to tuck tail and sulk about it? Fine. I'm not running an emotional support group here, Carla. This is DreadBall. He can sit while others, who understand that, play."

Bullseye shook her head. "That's a stupid thing to say."

He pulled away from her grip and leaned in close. "Yeah? Well, maybe you should sit, too. Maybe you should hit the showers."

The look on her face said everything Leeland needed to know: if she were holding a rifle, its reticle would be set right between his eyes. He hadn't seen her this mad—ever.

"Be careful, Leeland," Bullseye said, stepping back a pace. "Be careful."

He turned from her and felt the anger about everything that was going on in his life rising to his face. He wanted to hit the showers himself, forget the whole thing. Instead, he shouted, "Kirkus Tetsudo! Get your butt in there and win this game for us!"

***

Whoa! Was that an argument I just saw between Coach Roth and Bullseye Bock? One wonders what they were shouting at each other about. Game strategy, I suppose. One thing's for sure: Leeland's got bigger cajones *than me, getting up in her face like that. It's a wonder she didn't haul off and slap him. Stay tuned, my friends. We've got drama on—and off—the pitch.*

***

Me-Shan Lo took the ball on the hop and made a quick step into the strike zone. An Oceanic guard threw a fist toward his face. The jack ducked it easily, rifled the ball into the goal, and the Vipers went up by one.

Confetti cannons sounded at intervals around the arena as the first two rows of fans were covered with red and gold glitter. The announcer's booming voice sounded across the pitch. Red and gold lights reflected off the confetti and bathed the entire arena in bright, sparkling color.

The ball was shot back into play, and the Oceanics were on it.

A thin wiry striker named Kulani took the ball into his electromagnetic scoop and ran toward the Vipers' back goal. Given the striker's size, it was a wonder how he could manage to lug around that scoop on his arm. Festooned with scary-looking spikes and sharp edges, it was almost twice the size of a Corporation scoop. But this Sphyr striker was faster than any other Oceanic on the pitch. His speed caught Little Frankie and Me-Shan Lo by surprise, who tried stumbling backward to give pursuit. Dillon Koch turned and chased after him as well, but Kulani was too fast.

Kirkus Tetsudo, who had just entered the pitch, moved to intercept the speedy Oceanic, but he lacked the experience that Jerold Minata had and thus moved too fast and too close. Their move toward one another reminded Leeland of two mighty galaxies destined to strike. Had it been two guards, their impact might have shaken the arena. Instead, being strikers, Kirkus tried stealing the ball. Kulani simply shifted his lithe body slightly to the right and left Kirkus stumbling forward like a back alley drunk. Little Frankie made one final attempt at stealing the ball, but Kulani slid into a three-point position and fired it into the goal.

The Oceanics went up by two, and time was running out.

Leeland could feel Jimbo's eyes on his back, Bullseye's angry eyes on the side of his face. He ignored them both and shouted, "Frankie! Get that ball!"

Little Frankie heeded the words of his coach, raced back toward the center line, and found the ball at the mid-point in full spin and howl. He took it right in the chest but turned just in time for the hit to be glancing. The ball spun off his armor and into his glove. He remained upright and moved to score.

Maddog plowed the field before his striker, pushing an Oceanic jack and guard aside as if they were straw. Leeland could almost feel the rage inside his guard as Bullseye, beside him once again, issued full-throated commands at her player. Maddog was doing well, and Little Frankie stepped into the two-point strike zone to score.

Suddenly, Fat Coral, returning from the Sin Bin, was in Maddog's face. Where he had come from was anyone's guess, all blubber and muscle and dripping brackish water off his cleaved head. He took Maddog down with one punch, rudely stepped over his body, and jumped toward Little Frankie's legs.

The Viper striker tried jumping and firing the ball into the goal at the same time. He failed both. Fat Coral took Frankie in the knees just as he released the ball. The ball hit the goal and bounced away.

***

Oooohhh! What a shot! Maddog is down! Little Frankie is down! Time is running out. What's Leeland Roth going to do now to bring hope to his fans?

***

Leeland waved rookie guard Cyrus Voh into the fray to replace Maddog. He hesitated calling rookie Rollin Peck's name for Frankie.

Jimbo Threpe stood nearby, an arrogant little grin on his face, his helmet in hand and ready. Bullseye glared daggers at Leeland as well but said nothing.

Leeland shook his head, stifled an urge to scream, and thumbed Jimbo in. "Helmet up, you arrogant little—... Get us a score."

Jimbo slapped his helmet into place and took to the pitch.

The crowd erupted as they heard Jimbo's name echo across the arena, and he wasted no time moving to steal the ball.

Kulani had it again, but his good fortune didn't last long, as newly arrived Cyrus Voh, eager to show the crowd a little sizzle, knocked the Oceanic striker off his feet. He moved to stomp Kulani's head, but then backed off when the referee, who had been relatively silent all game, stepped into view.

Jimbo Threpe ignored the referee and followed the ball. On three bounces, he scooped it into his glove and moved to score.

Jacks Me-Shan Lo and Lucas Buck aided their star striker by trying to clear his path, but Fat Coral's watery blood was racing. He stepped into their path and took Me-Shan Lo down and drove him into the far wall. Lucas answered that insult against his fellow teammate by driving his fist into the face of a nearby Oceanic jack who tried the same on him. Lucas was then swept aside by a second Oceanic guard who blew into view and then faded away as Jimbo, unphased by any of it, kept his eyes and purpose fixed on the Oceanics' back goal. Down by two, a tie score wouldn't do it for them. With so many players moving into and out of the Sin Bin, what chance would the Vipers have of pulling it out in overtime?

Jimbo dodged a steal attempt, almost lost the ball on a second try. He pulled his glove to his chest to secure the hold, dodged a half-baked attempt of another Oceanic striker trying to restrain him illegally, and slipped into the back strike zone.

Fat Coral moved to intercept, but his ecstatic zeal and weight carried him too far. Jimbo allowed the brute to skip off his hip and fall hard to the pitch.

Jimbo drew the ball back, waited to allow the crowd's fervor to reach its zenith, then fired the ball into the goal.

The end-game buzzer sounded, and the Vitala Vipers won by a point.

Chapter 14

"I must say," Le Zuan Carooda said as he and Manan left Viper arena in a black, nondescript hover car that pulled into traffic and lost itself among the on-coming vehicles, "Jimbo Threpe is a fine, fine player. Makes the Vipers quite competitive. Wouldn't you agree?"

Manan nodded and accepted a small snifter of brandy from the beady-eyed little Judwan servant sharing the cab. He took a sip and winced at the strong taste. "He is, but that isn't what interests me at present. Leeland's hostility on the sidelines is what caught my eye."

"Yes," Le Zuan said, accepting a snifter of brandy himself. Unlike Manan, he took a larger sip and savored the strong flavor as he rolled the dark liquid across his tongue. "It would seem that our campaign of discredit is having an effect on Coach Roth's concentration. In the end, it did no lasting harm today, but in time, it will."

Manan risked another sip, cleared his throat, and said, "Perhaps we should increase the effort, put more rumors out there. Hit him with everything you have in your bag of tricks."

Le Zuan finished the brandy and handed the empty snifter to his assistant. He wiped a dew of moisture from his pale lips. "That would be unwise. The Mu'Shen'Wan teaches us patience and restraint in all behavior, all actions. If we unleash—forgive the pun—an ocean of accusations now, even the media will begin to question the validity of them. Now, they are willing to chase the shiny object, but only one at a time. Patience, my impetuous human companion. The season is long. We have plenty of time."

Le Zuan could see the frustration on the human's face. He continued. "Your concern now is two-fold. My sources tell me that your cousin, Aryan Kapoor, is sniffing around, trying to find the source of the leaks."

Manan finished off the brandy and handed his snifter over, refusing another. "I'm aware of his meddling. His sister has informed me of it. It's of no concern. Aryan is a cretin, a sniveling little back-alley drinker who got his position from his daddy's money and death."

Le Zuan nodded, though he knew, in his long experience, even sniveling back-alley drunkards could, on occasion, rise to pose a threat. "You should also be concerned that your friendly, half-blind assassin, Cegrich Wick, may not be planning the hit you and your client desire."

Manan raised his brow. "What are you talking about?"

"I hear that perhaps his target is not Jimbo Threpe, but maybe someone else on the team."

"Who?"

Le Zuan shrugged. "Who can say? If true, it may or may not have the same effect that you want. But the Mu'Shen'Wan also teaches us that deviation from a clear path, a clear goal, is fraught with danger. One misplaced bullet, my friend, can be the death of your plans."

He let his comment linger in the air between them, watching as Manan's mouth twitched with agitation, his brow wrinkle in uncertainty. Finally, Le Zuan tapped the side of the car, and the chauffeur took them down to street level, parked on a curb, and opened the door.

"This is where I leave you, Manan," Le Zuan said, moving his legs slightly to give the human a clear path out. "I wish you well until our next meeting."

Manan nodded and climbed out. Le Zuan tapped the side again, the door closed, and the car lifted and drifted back into traffic.

"A most disagreeable fellow, wouldn't you say?" Le Zuan asked his assistant.

The Judwan nodded. "Most. And he didn't like the brandy."

"Ah, humans lack good taste... and good instincts." He adjusted his seat, cleared his throat, accepted another snifter of brandy, and said, "Is it true? Conner Newberg is looking for a Judwan monk to train his players?"

His assistant nodded. "Yes, indeed. He's been contacting every Judwan he can find in Rosaria. He wants a Mu'Shen'Wan monk to prepare the Vipers for their second game against the Pelgar Mystics."

Le Zuan downed the brandy in one gulp, tossed the snifter to the floor, and barked, "The arrogance of humans! Thinking that they can buy a Judwan to betray its own people. So be it. Let's give him what he wants, shall we? Contact Remome, and make sure he gets the job."

The assistant nodded. "Yes, Le Zuan. It will be done."

As the call was made, Le Zuan laid back in his seat, closed his eyes, and allowed the brandy to work its magic.

Chapter 15

Viper Arena and Training Complex

Aryan Kapoor's exhaustion after sliding across two spheres and entering the Hope system was in full stride on his sleeping face. Leeland had asked for a late-night meeting shortly after the boy had arrived, to bring him quickly up to speed on what was going on in and around the Viper organization. As they discussed issues, Aryan fell asleep on the couch; Leeland left him there all night.

Leeland kicked Aryan's dangling shoe to wake him. "Up, Mr. Kapoor. Up!"

Aryan rolled to the left and fell off the couch, hitting the office floor. "Ouch!" he said, rubbing his hip, still half asleep. He shielded his eyes from the strong Hope sun that flooded into the room after Leeland pushed a button and the blinds slid open. "What time is it?"

"Time for the morning meeting," Leeland said. "Lots to do in the land of the living."

Despite his better judgment, Leeland was feeling good. Right now, the Vipers were three and one. Not a bad place to be halfway to the mid-point. Twelve games left. Anything, of course, could happen between now and the end of the season. But right now, the Vipers were cruising to a positive midseason record, and in the last couple days, the press had turned some of its sheep-like attention away from the brewing scandals and refocused its camera lens on what the Vipers were doing on the pitch. That, at the end of the day, was what truly mattered.

Bullseye, Conner, and Shapshir entered the office. The Asterian carried a tray of warm coffee and tea. Leeland smiled. The day was off to a good start.

"Welcome to Rosaria, Aryan," Bullseye said as she took her normal chair in front of Leeland's desk and grabbed a coffee. "Get your butt up and join the fun."

Aryan groaned and, finally, with much effort, climbed to his feet. He rubbed his face vigorously and shook his head. "I smell tea. Is that tea I smell?"

Shapshir nodded and handed the Viper owner a steaming cup. "Yes, sir, and may I welcome you to Rosaria as well."

Aryan took the drink and nodded. "Thank you." He took a sip and sighed such that Leeland thought he had melted back into sleep. Aryan closed his eyes and stood there a moment, basking in the warm aromatic steam rolling up from the teacup. He opened his eyes. "Where do I sit?"

"You can have my chair," Leeland said, pulling it out from his desk. "I prefer standing today."

Leeland tried flashing a smile at Bullseye, but she avoided eye contact, still sore, he supposed, after his bad behavior during the last game. He had tried a couple times to apologize, but things kept getting in the way. "Okay, let's get started. There's much to discuss."

Everyone took seats, and Leeland began. "Before our beloved leader fell asleep, I brought him up to speed on everything. We now sit at three games to one."

"Yeah," Aryan said, yawning and taking another sip, "Jimbo came through at the last minute." He chuckled. "If he keeps playing this well, he'll request a restructuring of his contract. Maybe you should sit him down for a game or two."

"He tried," Bullseye said, throwing a glance at Leeland. "It didn't work very well."

Again, Leeland didn't take the bait. He gestured toward Conner. "What's our personnel situation look like?"

Conner tapped a few buttons on his tablet. "I've got interviews scheduled this week with Boris Gerbock and Binnis Kahn."

Leeland raised an eyebrow. "Boris and Binnis? They're both pretty old."

Conner nodded. "Yeah, but if we can get one season out of them, it'll be worth it. They're good, solid jacks. Our rookies would thrive under their guidance."

"How's Frankie?"

Bullseye shook her head. "Over all, fine. He'll miss a couple games, but he'll be back before the midseason break."

Leeland pointed to Shapshir. "I want to go visit with him later today. You come with me?"

Shapshir nodded. "Absolutely."

Leeland tapped his desk's dashboard display. Game video appeared on the wall to their right. "Our next opponent: the Boolean Cragsmen, a Forge Father team that doesn't impress me over much. Nothing about them seems unique. They do rely heavily on MVPs, it would seem, hiring them often. That's something we'll need to keep an eye on, watch for the announcement of whom they may hire against us. Otherwise, I'll be recommending our standard lineup in the team meeting this afternoon. This will be another home game, so we have that advantage as well."

They took a few minutes to watch the video. The Cragsmen were facing an Ada-Lorana team and were getting thoroughly trounced.

"Yes," Bullseye said, "they seem pretty workmen-like in their approach to the game. But you know as well as I do, Leeland, that a Forge Father team is never to be taken lightly."

Bullseye hadn't called him 'Leelee' since the last game, despite several opportunities to do so. Another sign that all was not well between them. The bright, sunny, cheerful morning was growing cloudy. "I never take Forge Fathers lightly, Carla."

The moment of silence ended with Shapshir bringing up the gorilla in the room. "Coach Roth, I must ask that we discuss a few non-team, non-game-related issues."

Leeland rolled his eyes. "There goes my pleasant morning..."

"I ask—no, I must *insist*—that you hold a press conference this week. Right now, the FSIDL is taking a hands-off approach to all the accusations surrounding your brother. But that will not last unless you put yourself in front of the press and answer questions, no matter how difficult they may be."

"Didn't the GCPS and Digby lawyers get enough information out of me to put all this stupidity to rest?"

Shapshir nodded. "You were very fulsome in your responses at the inquiry, yes. But there's mounting pressure on FSIDL to, at a minimum, open their own investigation and even suspend you until the truth of it all rises to the surface. And, given your outburst on the sideline in the last game—"

"Son of a Zee!" Leeland shouted, making Aryan start and nearly spill his tea. "There's *never* been a time in all the history of DreadBall that a coach hasn't blown up on the sidelines?"

"Yes, sir, you are right. It happens all the time. But the context here is what matters. People are beginning to think that your outburst was caused by the stress related to the scandal, the investigations."

"And they wouldn't be wrong," Bullseye said, glaring at Leeland across the desk.

"Very powerful special interests here in Rosaria," Shapshir continued, "are beginning to wonder if perhaps Coach Roth should be replaced with a more stable figure."

"Well," Leeland said in the most sarcastic tone he could muster, "here's your chance, Conner. You're the coach now. Knock yourself out."

"Don't be stupid, Leelee," Bullseye said, finally using her patented term of endearment. "You're the coach of the Vipers. No one else."

"And this is the reason petitions are being signed to change the team's name," Shapshir said. He shook his head and puckered his lips as if he were going to whistle. Instead, he said, "Whoever is behind all this sure has a long, long reach."

Leeland paused before saying anything else. He breathed deeply, letting his anger, his frustration, subside. Then, he said, "Why don't you bring everyone up to speed, Aryan, on what you've learned?"

Aryan leaned up in his chair and took a final sip of tea. "Well, it's Saanvi for sure. I visited her right before coming here. She didn't admit her involvement, but there's no doubt in my mind. She's not capable of leaving the prison, but she still has many, many connections within our corporation. Her contact on this issue is a sniveling little cousin of mine named Manan. I'm certain of it. He's the proverbial black sheep of the family."

Bullseye chuckled. "I thought you filled that role."

"My wool is silver-blond compared to his." He shot a glance at Leeland. "I may be a recovering drunk and playboy. He's Kali incarnate. The rumors about him are legion."

Conner shook his head. "He has that many connections in the First Sphere that he can cause all this trouble?"

"No," Aryan said. "He's the conduit through which Saanvi's message gets delivered. He's working with someone, some organization. Who or what that is, I don't know."

"This information should be given to the lawyers," Shapshir said. "And law enforcement."

Aryan nodded, cleared his throat. "Yes, and I'd like you to accompany me when I do. I'll avail myself for any further questions they may have. I also want to make it clear that, now that I'm here, all non-gameplay, administrative matters, flow through me. I'll take over the day-to-day running of our operation here."

Leeland couldn't help but, again, be impressed. The boy had come so far and so quickly. If his father, Daman Kapoor, were still alive, perhaps he'd be proud. Aryan was certainly showing the kind of maturity that might, in time, allow him to reclaim control of Kapoor Industries. Maybe, if Saanvi didn't get in his way.

"So," Shapshir said, rising from his chair, "when can I schedule a press conference?"

Never! That's what Leeland wanted to say, but all eyes were on him. "Fine. Schedule it for tomorrow afternoon. I'll answer every question the little zits have. Meeting adjourned."

He walked to the door.

"Where are you going?" Aryan asked. "There are some other matters we need to dis—"

"I'm going to the field. I need some practice."

***

Leeland hadn't suited up since the Third Sphere tournament finals. His broken ribs, and all the other injuries he had suffered in that game, had healed and were no longer a problem. Well, no longer a problem on paper, though he still felt the occasional tweak of pain if he twisted the wrong way or sat down in one position for too long. The signs of aging, he knew. Contractually, he had agreed to never again set foot onto a pitch as a player for the Vitala Vipers. There was nothing in the contract, however, that said he couldn't practice on his own.

The cannon fired the ball down the center line. Leeland extended the electromagnetic scoop on his glove and caught it on the fly.

The three strike zones on the opponent's side of the pitch were active. Leeland tucked the ball into his body, as he used to do as a player to avoid steals, and moved to score. He dodged invisible guards and jacks, extended his left hand as if he were strong-arming a thieving striker. He stepped into the strike zone, considered a two-point shot, but moved ahead three steps and fired the ball toward the goal.

Miss!

Not surprising. Other than score practice with his strikers, he hadn't thrown a ball since the tournament finals. He was as rusty as a discarded Lancer battle tank on a forgotten field of war. The muscles in his arm strained against the throw. And now, he'd have to run after the ball.

His cardio was still in good shape. Endurance had never been an issue in his career, even after leaving the game in disgrace after Victor's death. His time in the Xtreme DreadBall arena had actually improved his breathing technique and had given him an almost sixth sense on where the ball might bounce after a failed score attempt. His skills did not fail him now.

The ball bounced into the Vipers' side of the pitch, but all of those strike zones and goals were inactive. It struck the nearest goal on bounce and ricocheted right into Leeland's waiting glove.

He turned immediately, this time not worrying about protecting the ball. He was moving a la Mackinaw Jim in a kind of carefree manner, pretending to let his aura, his personality and ego, lead him to score. It was silly, and Leeland felt foolish preening his neck and waving to an empty stadium. But he drew energy from it, imagining that he was, like Jimbo, at the height of his career, ten years ago when both he and Victor were relative newcomers to the game. The accolades were sweet back in those days. Now, for any personal accolades he might receive, he felt honor-bound to share them with his players. They were the reason the Vipers were three and one right now. They were the reason he got up every morning and put on his coach's hat. They were the reason he didn't just walk away from it all, turn his back to it, and find some quiet corner of the galaxy to put down roots. *Someday...*

He slid into the strike zone and fired the ball into the goal. Score!

Heather's clapping echoed across the pitch. "Very good, Leeland. You've still got it."

"Duck!" He screamed.

At first, Heather balked, not understanding what Leeland was ordering her to do. The cannon fired. Leeland shouted again, this time with hand motions for her to step back. Heather stiffened, took a step back, and Leeland reached across her body and caught the ball before it struck her in the shoulder.

He slid across the pitch, the ball sending sparks flying as it scraped the floor. "Shut it down!" Leeland screamed. "Shut it down!"

The strike zones deactivated, the cannon and the ball fell silent. Leeland lay there a moment, catching his breath and wits. Then, he stood, straightened his uniform, and let the ball drop from his glove.

"I'm sorry, Leeland, I—"

"Never step onto a live DreadBall pitch without armor," he said, in a voice harsher and more scolding than he wanted. Leeland removed his helmet and wiped his brow. "That was close."

"I'm sorry, I... I didn't know."

She seemed near tears. Leeland dropped his helmet and offered her his hand. "That's okay, Heather. It's my fault. I should have locked the gate to keep anyone from wandering onto the pitch." He smiled. "I certainly didn't expect you'd pay me a visit."

Heather let Leeland guide her to the Viper bench. "I only came because I wanted to see how you were doing. Bullseye said you were here 'burning off steam,' as she put it."

Leeland chuckled. "Yeah, that sounds like Bullseye. She's not wrong. The last couple of weeks have been stressful, I admit."

"Are you worried about your next game?"

He nodded. "I'm always worried about that. But no. It's the rumor mill grinding Victor's good name into dust."

To Heather, Victor's 'good name' was a relative term, Leeland figured. He wished he could rephrase his answer, but she gave him no time. "And your name too, I gather?"

Leeland shrugged. "I can handle the press. But how are you doing? I haven't had an opportunity to come check on you guys recently."

"We're fine. Trying to stay busy. A little bored."

Leeland understood that, especially since she and Vicky were trying their best to steer clear of the media. Not too difficult when in the complex, but the press was always camped out in front of every escape route. "Well, our last two games are away games. You and Vicky are more than welcome to accompany us."

Heather paused. She shot a quick smile at him as if she were searching for the right words or the right way to say them. "The next game is what I actually came to talk to you about."

"Oh?"

"Yes. Vicky would like to be with you, on the sidelines, if that is okay?"

Leeland leaned back and considered the proposal. He couldn't recall any Digby rules that specifically prevented family members from being on the sidelines with the coaching staff. Then again, he couldn't recall any instances when he was a Trontek 29er, where sons or daughters or spouses of players were on the sidelines. "I don't know, Heather. I'm not sure it's a good idea. It's not about her physical safety. She'd be safe in that regard. But things can get heated on the sidelines. Foul language, foul behavior. It may not be a good environment for a child."

Heather huffed and shook her head. "She's not a delicate flower, Leeland. She's young, yes, but she's tougher than you know." She winked. "She's got Roth blood in her, remember? This would be a good opportunity to spend more time with her. It would be good for her; she's restless. And... maybe good for you too?"

Leeland pulled back. "Good for me? How would having a child on the sidelines be—" A light went off in his head. "Wait... this is Bullseye's idea, isn't it?"

Heather looked down at her shoes as if the answer were written on the laces. "Well—"

"Gah! That woman!"

She put her hand on his arm. "Don't be mad at her, Leeland. She worries about you. She loves you."

"Loves me? She's old enough to be my mother. My grandmother."

"Not like that, you goon. Like a sister, a mother. She's worried about your mental state..."

Leeland thought back on the tournament when Bullseye had gone totally bonkers over Triple-B's terrible death, how she had left the team and had even taken a coaching position on another team that played against the Vipers' march toward the championship. *Now, she worries about* my *mental health? That woman!*

"...and your public image."

That, Leeland had to admit, was a concern. Talk in the media about replacing him as the Viper coach and the petition to have the team's name changed to suit the local audience were serious concerns, and ones that, if allowed to persist, would begin to affect his players. Thinking about them for a moment, Leeland realized how well they had been handling the controversy. But if the coach of the Vipers kept exploding on the sidelines, regardless of the reason, those calls for change would translate into loss after loss after loss.

Perhaps I should agree, Leeland considered, *if for no other reason but as a way to apologize to Bullseye*. He hadn't figured out any other way yet.

"Okay," he said, standing, "Vicky can stand on the sidelines with me, so long as she behaves herself, and doesn't show me up by calling better plays."

Heather laughed, stood, and whisked a lock of hair out of her face. "Very well. I'll speak to her about both conditions, but I'm not making any promises."

They laughed together, and Leeland took a moment to stare into her eyes. Dark, pretty, hopeful.

He pointed toward the locker room. "I have to catch a shower, but afterward, would you and Vicky care to have lunch with me? I know a wonderful seafood place a few blocks away. They roast an excellent Rosaria River Shark. Melts in your mouth."

Heather nodded, "But, what about the press?"

Leeland waved her off. "Don't worry about that. I have an Asterian assistant who can divert the media's attention for at least a good hour."

Chapter 16

Leeland suppressed the urge to shout obscenities at rookie striker Rollin Peck as he, once again, found the Sin Bin on a poor decision. The young man had good speed and good pickpocketing skills, but his judgment on a score attempt was abysmal. Like his mentor Jimbo, he worked too much showmanship into the attempt, preening for the cameras as if he were a swan or... well, Jimbo. Neither was true and thus, his scoring method exposed too much of his body. The Boolean Cragsmen took advantage.

"I told you to stop doing that," Leeland barked as the medibot hauled Rollin to the Sin Bin. "Didn't I tell you to stop doing that?"

Rollin raised a shaking hand but didn't speak. Leeland waved him away. "Go, get out of my sight, you—"

Vicky was at his side. Leeland checked his words. "Good... good." He clapped his hands. "Let's go. Let's go. Boris, you're up."

They had settled on Boris Gerbock as Artemis Hale's replacement. Boris was a veteran who didn't seem to stick anywhere. He'd played all over the First Sphere for many different Corporate teams. Now at the end of his career, he had signed a four-game deal with the Vipers, with agreement for future considerations if his time proved valuable. At this moment, Leeland couldn't really see any value with putting the old man on the pitch for any other reason than filling a spot on a quickly dwindling team.

"You should give Me-Shan the ball," Vicky said as the roar of the crowd dwindled to a nearly untraceable volume. The fans, like the Vipers, were too quiet today.

"What?" Leeland asked.

"Let Me-Shan have the ball." She glanced at the pitch. "He's not a very good defender."

Me-Shan had been working the defense more than controlling the ball. A very necessary role given that the ball had been on the Viper side of the pitch most of the game. Now down by two with time running out, perhaps Me-Shan did look silly holding back.

"Conner," Leeland said, "send your striker-jack after the ball."

Conner nodded and shouted directions at his player. Me-Shan nodded happily and moved.

Boom!

The crowd gave a collective groan as Jimbo, who was trying for the ball as well, went down under a strong slam by a Cragsmen guard who had already sent three Vipers into the Sin Bin. The ball skipped out of reach, and Me-Shan Lo went after it.

The Viper jack had difficulty finding the ball on bounce—it seemed erratic today, as if some hacker had fiddled with its internal guidance system. Earlier, the game had been paused to check that out. No tampering found. It was just one of those days where nothing seemed to go right for the Vipers.

The ball bounced off the helmet of Shadrack, who lost his footing and fell. Me-Shan jumped over the big man, extended his scoop, and caught the ball on the fly.

Down the pitch he ran, faster than a jack had a right to move. Any lingering questions that the media might still have about Me-Shan's athleticism exceeding that of any jack player would now be put to rest, as the fast, agile man moved in such a way as to give Leeland goosebumps.

Shadrack went down in a hail of Forge Father fists. Now, only four Vipers players remained standing on the pitch. Time was running out, and Me-Shan was alone.

"Go! Go!" Leeland shouted, waving his arms toward the nearest Cragsmen goal.

The jack held the ball tightly against his chest, spun three-sixty around the Cragsmen MVP, a stout, burly fellow that Leeland had never seen before. Me-Shan left the brute in the proverbial dust, stepped over Spencer Mills who had just been slammed down in his path, and slid into scoring position.

The crowd now came to life, both sides. Vipers fans were shouting and stomping their feet such that the arena shook. Red and gold lights were flashing. The big screens above the pitch, showing every angle of the game, all refocused on Me-Shan's position.

For their part, the small, but enthusiastic Cragsmen fans shouted their patented slogan, "True-false-true-false," which Leeland had yet to figure out, though he figured it had something to do with their name. The arena pulsed with energy as all eyes turned to Me-Shan Lo.

The Vipers jack stepped into the two-point position, arched his back, and readied for the throw. A Cragsmen jack tried a futile leap to knock Me-Shan away from the score attempt, only to be throttled by Dillon Koch and ridden to the wall. Me-Shan adjusted his position in the strike zone, reared his arm back, and threw the ball.

Score!

Leeland, Conner, and Vicky embraced as time ran out. Tie game. Now, they would go into overtime, and—

Wait! What was this? The crowd's jubilation suddenly turned to angry shouts and moans. Leeland turned his head and stared at the screens above the arena.

The game was not going into overtime, for Me-Shan Lo was awarded only one point for the score.

Planet Gaylor

Manan waited impatiently for Cegrich Wick to arrive. He wiggled his nose against the inhospitable air of the unventilated room that he had been led into to await the Veer-myn's arrival. *How dare this cretin make me wait,* he thought as he paced back and forth to the rumble of an Xtreme DreadBall match being played in the sewers nearby. Very nearby, in fact. The walls of the room were so thin that Manan could hear the ball striking the other side. If just one crack developed from one of those strikes… well, foul, diseased-ridden water would fill the room. Manan felt for the transmitter in his pocket. *Keep me waiting much longer, Cegrich Wick, and see what happens.*

The warped, moss-riddled door to the room opened. An aging, stooped Veer-myn entered.

"You aren't The Whip," Manan said. "Where is he? I did not pay him such a large sum to be kept waiting."

The Veer-myn, clothed in a tattered red robe and a loose white undergarment, said, "My apologies, but Cegrich Wick is, at the moment, occupied. His team is playing the Fellspur Corruption, as I'm sure you can hear through the walls. He will not be able to attend to you today. But is there anything I can help you with?"

Manan suppressed the urge to bite his lip and activate his transmitter. He fought the urge to pull the pistol he had tucked away in his boot and fire it at the grinning fool in front of him. *Le Zuan is right; this punk is taking me for a ride.* "Very well. Tell your master that time is running out on the job I've paid him to do. The Vipers have just concluded their fifth game. Only three games remain before the midseason break, and our agreement was clear: Jimbo Threpe *must* be dead before the break, or the deal is off, and the money will disappear from his account. Does he understand that?"

The Veer-myn dared take a step toward Manan. He held his long, clawed hands forward in peace. "I can assure you, sir, that Cegrich Wick understands the agreement well, and he wants to *assure you* that an attempt on Jimbo Threpe will come soon. Very soon."

Manan shook his head. "An *attempt* isn't the agreement. Instruct your master that he will not play word games with me. There are no loopholes in our agreement. The Viper striker must *die* by the midseason break. A mere attempt will not suffice."

Manan stepped forward. He pulled his pistol from his boot and held it against his leg as he approached the old, withered rodent. The Veer-myn stepped back against the wall looking left then right as if he were searching for an escape route.

Manan leaned in close enough to smell the creature's foul breath. "Give Mr. Wick one final word for me, please. Inform him that, not only will the money dry up, but if he fails in his mission, it will be the last mission that he ever conducts. Do you understand?"

The Veer-myn shook his body in agreement. "Yes, sir. I will convey your message to my mas—to Cegrich Wick."

Manan stepped back, nodded, and tucked his pistol away. "Good. You tell him all that. And tell him... I'll be watching."

Chapter 17

Viper Arena and Training Complex

An official appeal was made to Digby about their final score against the Boolean Cragsmen, and it was denied. Slo-mo vid footage showed Me-Shan Lo, on his last adjustment, had two-thirds of his left foot outside the two-point strike zone, and the ruling was clear: a player's feet had to be 'inside' the two-point zone to count. One point was given, and therefore, the Cragsmen won the game by a point.

"There's nothing more that we can do about it," Leeland said as he and the entire team, including Aryan, gathered in the meeting room to discuss a wide variety of topics. "Their ruling is final."

"That's ridiculous!" Me-Shan Lo said, clearly upset with the ruling, with himself, with the universe. "We must appeal the ruling."

Aryan, who sat between Bullseye and Conner, shook his head. "I've explored those options, but the FSIDL is taking the vid evidence as solid. They are satisfied that there was no tampering with the footage, nothing doctored. It's an official clip from the game. We can go through the motions of an appeal, but the ruling will, in the end, stand."

Leeland couldn't help but wonder if Me-Shan's frustration was not only due to his poor judgment in the final seconds of the throw, but due to the controversy surrounding his status on the team as a de facto jack-striker. It was obvious to anyone with eyes that the Viper strikers, even the rookies, gave Me-Shan the cold shoulder. Missing a two-pointer that would have tied the game gave them even further ammunition to reject him as 'one of their own.' So far, their lack of respect (jealousy, perhaps?) for Me-Shan hadn't come to a boil nor had Conner indicated otherwise. Leeland made a mental note to keep a sharp eye on matters and immediately tamp down any unhealthy rivalries that might arise among his players.

"So, that's that," he said, turning away from that issue and starting the meeting. "We're three and two, with three games left before the midseason break." He raised a finger. "If we win at least one of our next three games, we have a good shot at making the Ultimate match."

Dillon Koch raised his hand, and Leeland recognized him. "If I may ask, Boss, what's the benefit of playing that game? The mid-break is three full weeks. If we play that game, we only have two weeks off. An extra week of no games would go a long way in getting everyone back to health."

Many turned their heads toward Little Frankie, who was still nursing leg wounds from their game against the Nemion Oceanics. He was scheduled to sit out their next game, but everyone knew that he needed more time. Everyone but Frankie, of course, who wanted to dive right back in. But this morning, Leeland detected something else in the striker's demeanor. Not just fatigue; they were all tired in one way or another. No. Something in Frankie's eyes, as he avoided contact with all who stared at him, was most worrisome.

"You're right," Leeland said, turning back to Dillon. "Another full week would go a long way in healing wounds. There's also the adverse effect of going cold. Too much time off can allow lethargy to set in, and that can be just as devastating.

"The benefits of playing in the Ultimate match are myriad," he continued, "one of which is exposure. A first-season, Third Sphere up-start playing well enough to enter that match? That's important exposure that will pay off in spades down the road. Another benefit is that we'll be playing for charity. That too helps to shine a positive light on the organization. A positive light which we need right now."

Nobody in the room spoke to that, but Leeland could see what they were all thinking: *a positive light needed because of your and Victor's scandals*. None of the players on the team had suffered any controversies to date. They were all behaving themselves, and that wasn't easy, Leeland knew. Dillon Koch was known for hitting the drink and getting into fights. Jimbo was a notorious ladies' man. The Maddog had a gambling problem. Shadrack was a recovering drug addict. Everyone on the team had a so-called 'dark side.' None of them were perfect human beings. That didn't bother Leeland, for he was the least perfect of them all.

Jimbo piped in. "The problem I see with that game is that, with four teams on the pitch, there is four times the likelihood of being slammed to paste."

Conner cleared this throat. "Possibly, but not necessarily. Ultimate match rules will be in place but, this being a game for charity, the FSIDL does not want it to be the kind of bloody engagement that we often see in such four-team brawls. Fouls will be strictly enforced. And they have also asked that all teams field small line-ups: only one guard per team on the pitch at a time."

Shadrack raised his hand. "Do we know who our competition might be if we get in?"

Leeland shrugged and tapped buttons on the podium. A team grid of the two FSIDL conferences and their four divisions hung three-dimensional in the air.

"Nothing affirmative right now," he said. "The top team from each division will play. The Bremlin Nebulas and the Trontek 29ers are fighting it out right now atop the Sol

Division. In our own Hope division, it is us and the Oceanics. In the Radner Division of the Star Conference, the Metabot Daring Circuits are all but walking away with it, though the Void Sirens are nipping at their metal heels."

Leeland shot a quick glance at Bullseye and saw her face light up with the possibility of her old team making the Ultimate match. It would be a nice treat for her to enjoy, but he wondered how she'd fare coaching against the Void Sirens.

"And finally, in the Cascadia Division, we have either the Asterian Shan-Meeg Starhawks or the Forge Father Midgard Delvers. All of these teams are most capable and will pose different challenges for us if we get in." He turned off the grid. "So, I say again, if we win one of our next three games, we have a good chance of making the match. If we win two, we have a very high chance. If we win all three, we're all but guaranteed."

"There are no guarantees in DreadBall, Boss," Spencer Mills said, getting chuckles from his teammates.

Leeland nodded. "Don't I know it! So, let's turn our attention now to our next opponent: The Koeputki Kolossals. The last time we played against a Zee team, I asked, how do we beat them? And someone said… 'Show up.'"

That received another round of laughter from the players. Leeland waited for it to die down, then said, "And indeed, that's part of it. But I will reiterate what I said for the Whitestar Chimps: don't take the Zee for granted. All jacks, all capable of slamming and scoring. Their slam capabilities don't concern me much, but they will endeavor to score. They slam in tandem to gain advantage. And they cheat. They'll foul us all up and down the pitch.

"We'll start with a 2-2-2 formation: two guards, two jacks, two strikers. For strikers, Jimbo and Spencer will start."

"For jacks," Conner chimed in, "Me-Shan Lo and Jerold."

"For guards," Bullseye said, "Maddog and Dillon."

Leeland tapped buttons on his podium, and a colorized DreadBall pitch appeared. He pressed his hand through the display and placed two G's, two J's, and two S's on the display to indicate where players would start. "I want both my guards and jacks up on the start line. Jimbo and Spencer, you'll set up back from the line a few paces, but not too far. When the ball is fired into play, let it fly down the center line, wait for it to pass, and then I want the guards and jacks to hit those little zits like a wall of iron. Turn them into slam fodder right away.

"Jimbo and Spencer will then move to catch the ball on ricochet and then score. I don't care if it's the front goals or the back one. If you're near a goal, strike it! Score, score, score. I want to *win this game* before the final rush."

Leeland paused to let his plan sink in. No one in the room spoke. Then he said, "Any questions?"

If anyone had them, they didn't speak up, nor did their expressions indicate concern or confusion of the plan. The plan was simple. Nothing about it should concern his players. The Zee should not be taken for granted, yes, but despite a few players nursing injuries, the Vipers lineup was solid. Solid and ready to go.

"Dismissed."

As they filed out of the room, Leeland tugged Little Frankie aside. "Hey, can we talk?"

Frankie nodded. "Sure, Boss, what's up?"

"That's the question I'll ask you: what's up, buddy? You seem distracted about something. Anything you'd like to share? What's on your mind?"

Frankie waited until everyone had left the room. Then, he sighed and whispered, "I'm worried about my health, Boss. This is the second long-term injury that's put me down. I'm beginning to wonder if I'm accident prone. I'm not sure I'm going to even last the season if this keeps up."

Leeland shook his head and shrugged. "DreadBall's a tough sport, Frankie. You know that."

"Yes, I know, but how long can I keep getting battered like this and remain viable? It's like I've got a bullseye on my back when I'm on the pitch."

Leeland suddenly got a silly image in his mind of Bullseye on his striker's back. He shook it away. "You should consider it an honor. Our opposition knows your worth. They know, if you stay on the field, you score."

Frankie shook his head. "My knees don't feel like it's an honor. Jimbo never suffers these kinds of injuries."

"Not true at all. Remember back in the tournament, he couldn't field against the Saltborne Sledgehammers. I had to take his place, remember?"

Frankie nodded. "Yes, yes, I know. But he bounces back so quickly."

"Well, everyone's constitution is different. Jimbo's got the luck of the Old Earth gods about him. I swear, I sometimes think he sold his soul to some malevolent spirit. But everyone gets banged up over time, son. It's the nature of the game."

Leeland placed his hand on Frankie's shoulder. "Look, you're one of the finest strikers I've had the pleasure to work with. You have a spark, a spirit, that's hard to find in players. Trust me, you'll have a long career. As long as mine, at least. You'll sit out against the Zee. We'll reassess your situation before we field against the Z'zor, okay? We'll make sure you're *ready* to play before you play."

That seemed to mollify Frankie's concerns, although Leeland could still see some self-doubt in the boy's eyes.

Frankie nodded. "Okay, Boss. Thanks."

Leeland slapped him on the shoulder. "Now, go and grab a bite to eat. We'll have striker practice in three hours. You won't field, but I want you there. Okay?"

"Okay."

***

The Vipers' fans seemed particularly rowdy this game. The unfortunate loss against the Cragsmen had not been forgotten. They screamed and shouted and barked and shook the Vipers arena in such a way as to take Leeland back to his early days as a 29er. *This* was the kind of audience that he remembered and welcomed. The visiting Kolossals fans, a small and tightly-packed retinue sitting in the stands behind the visitor's back goal, seemed meek by comparison.

And so too did their team.

Dillon Koch hooked a back-jumper by the ape's tiny arm and slammed it straight to the floor. The overworked medibot let the broken Zee jack lie there while the game continued. Jimbo stepped over the injured Zee and moved to score.

"Shoot that ball, you son of a—" Leeland checked his language and looked down. Oh right, Vicky wasn't beside him for this match. She'd decided to be with Bullseye in the coach's box. "Shoot the ball, you son of a Zee!"

Leeland couldn't decide if hurling such an insult had the same impact when one was playing against the Zee, given the fact that they were clones, sons of the petri dish. They might misconstrue it as a compliment. Leeland cupped his mouth again. "Just... score. Score!"

Jimbo was in rare form, having already scored twice and almost hitting the back goal with a three-pointer that would have ended the game early. That one missed, and the Zee had managed to trundle down the pitch and knock one in for two. Now the Vipers were up by two, and Jimbo had the ball.

A growling Zee had Jimbo by the leg. Another tried to jump on his back, but he turned just in time to allow Maddog to pop the overzealous monkey in the chops and put him down for good.

With a chimp on his calf, Jimbo moved into position to score. The Zee bit down hard on his Achilles heel. Even from his vantage point, Leeland could see Jimbo's body shake from the pain. He couldn't see blood, but it was there. One didn't get bitten by a Zee and not lose an ounce or two. But Jimbo steadied his stance, despite his pain, raised his glove, and hurled the ball at the goal.

Score!

The Vipers went up by three, and the ball was fired down the center line.

Jimbo hobbled across the pitch toward Leeland. Behind him, a mad scramble for the ball began.

"How bad is the bite?" Leeland asked as Jimbo fell to the floor beside him and took off his helmet.

The wounded striker gritted his teeth and revealed the tear in his uniform. As expected, there was blood, lots of it. "Hurts like a mother."

"Can you walk?"

Jimbo nodded.

"Go to the Sin Bin and have the medibot look at it," Leeland said. He pointed to Kirkus Tetsudo. "You're up!"

Kirkus put on his helmet and raced onto the pitch.

Little Frankie helped Jimbo to the Sin Bin, and Leeland noticed a small, cheerful smile on the boy's face. Just seeing Jimbo get injured, albeit a painful but mild wound, seemed to brighten the young man's spirits. Leeland knew that there was no malice in Frankie's joy. He didn't want to see Jimbo get injured any more than any other player. But seeing the mighty Mackinaw Jim get wounded was a good reminder that even the 'Golden Boy' was not invincible.

Kirkus was out of position to affect the ball scramble, but Spencer Mills was in the thick of it; everyone else was fighting for the little whizzing steel sphere of death.

The Zee always seemed to outnumber their opponents two to one. There were twice as many Zee fighting for the ball as there were Vipers, their tiny glove-clad hands, with their small, circular, pulsating electromagnetic scoops on top, reaching through the scramble, sparking against Spencer's and throwing his arm backward. For a moment, Leeland lost track of where his striker was.

Then Dillon Koch appeared on the perimeter of the brawl. The short, stocky guard threw a few jabs at the back of Zee heads. Bodies dropped, and Spencer emerged from the pile, ball in glove.

Kirkus now sprinted past the pile of recovering Zee bodies. Spencer shuffled the ball over to his teammate, who pretended to tuck and move, only to then shuffle it back to Spencer, who then shuffled it back to Kirkus.

Again and again, they passed the ball back and forth to each other, keeping the pursuing Zee confused and cross-eyed as to who had the ball at any given time. To Leeland, it seemed as if it didn't really matter to either one of his strikers who had the ball when the time came to put it into the goal. He was pleased. This was not a play that they had practiced, but it didn't matter. It was working, and he was so happy to see such unselfish play between his men.

The Zee tried to form a castle, but Spencer and Kirkus were moving too fast. A Zee slid haphazardly into Kirkus's line of sight, blocking a clear shot on the goal. He flicked the ball to Spencer, who was too close to the back goal for a four-pointer but didn't waste time.

Spencer paused, readied his throw, and put the ball into the goal over the short reach of Zee hands.

The Vipers were now up by six, and the ball was fired down the center line.

A Zee jack named Impen Tuck scooped it up on first bounce. The little chimp had scored once already, a slam dunk for a point. Now, Impen made a dash toward the Vipers' back goal.

Throughout the game, Bullseye had been conducting what Leeland would call a flex-castle, one created on the fly as soon as a Zee touched the ball. Ideally, it would be formed by jacks and guards, but oftentimes those fellows were down the pitch. Whoever was near the back goal at the time was required to defend it. This time, Jerold Minata and Maddog were up.

They pedaled back as the action on the pitch crested toward the Vipers' back goal. Everyone pursued Impen Tuck. Clearly, he was the fastest Zee on the Kolossals, and he made a point not to dawdle or play to the crowd. He was no Jimbo Threpe.

Spencer Mills caught up to the speedy Zee and tried a steal. Impen shifted to the right, using the referee's shiny metal body as a shield against the attempt. Spencer's foot caught the referee's. He stumbled and slammed his helmet right into the pitch. Kirkus tried a similar move, but Impen Tuck did a little frog leap that left his second human striker scraping the floor.

Now the only thing between Impen and the back goal were the castle defenders, neither of which were very skilled at the task.

Maddog held the spot right in front of the goal. Jerold wavered behind him, not sure which side of the strike zone he should protect. Impen gave him little to no security in that decision, bobbing and weaving through all attempts at bringing him down or dislodging the ball.

Kirkus tried one more try at a pickpocket, but Impen slid into the four-point spot in the strike zone, realized that Maddog held the interior line, took two steps to the right, another to the left, and threw the ball.

It was a fast spin that reminded Leeland of Jimbo's best tosses. Jerold leapt at the ball as it screamed toward the goal. Maddog put up a fist and missed a deflection by a centimeter. The ball now had an unfettered path to the goal.

A collective gasp spread through the crowd as they waited for the result.

The ball struck the goal, rattled around, and fell out.

Leeland could feel the tension of the moment fade as Vipers fans cheered and Kolossals fans wept.

Kirkus, being closest to the ball, scooped it up and tossed it to a waiting Spencer, his helmet visor sporting a large crack. Spencer caught the ball, turned, and moved to score.

"Come on, Spencer," Leeland shouted from the sidelines. "Take that shot!"

Spencer crossed the center line to the deafening sound of the crowd. Red and golden lights flashed through the arena. The vid screens along the walls and above the pitch showed Spencer's move from every angle, and it seemed to Leeland that all the attention was distracting his striker from his purpose. Unlike Jimbo, who would be eating the attention like chocolate, Spencer balked, slowed, and for a second, wasn't sure what to do.

Then he realized no one, not a single Zee, was chasing him. He sprinted again, this time with purpose, toward the closest goal.

He stepped into the two-point spot, but with no Zees on him or in pursuit, he simply trotted up to the goal and slammed the ball home.

The Vipers went up by seven, the game was called, and the Vipers crowd exploded.

Chapter 18

Troken, Desert Planet

The director of the SportsBlast commercial was a squirrely little fellow with a long beard and a thin mouth. "Cut! Cut!" he shouted through the voice augmenter strapped to his neck as star players from five different FSIDL teams went through the rigors of pretending to play DreadBall. About a dozen drones buzzed around the makeshift pitch, filming the action at every conceivable angle. Leeland stood on the sidelines sweating and cursing. This was the tenth time that the director had called 'cut' at this moment in the shoot. Nine too many times in Leeland's mind.

The day was drawing out, the heat was rising, and nerves were fraying. All but Jimbo seemed to be annoyed by the director's useless perfectionism. There was no crowd anywhere near the hard, sandy plateau on which they were filming. Jimbo played to them anyway.

The director's problem seemed to lie with the Kalyshi striker that the director had set up to try to steal the ball from Jimbo. The idea was that she'd come up at the last minute and swipe the ball from Jimbo and score instead. Well, not the ball, but a container of the new DreadMax sports drink that the SportsBlast Food and Drug Corporation was trying to market... *"Drink and feel fabulous until the final rush!"* Leeland wanted to puke all over that slogan, though he did have to admit that it was a tasty, revitalizing drink. Several bottles had already been downed by everyone on the set.

"Neela," the director said as he approached her on the pitch. A drone moved above the director to cast shade as he walked out into the squelching heat toward Jimbo and the Kalyshi. "You need to steal the bottle with your left arm. That's the side that's going to be facing the camera."

The up-and-coming Bremlin Nebulas player threw up her arms and groaned. "Last cut, you said the right!"

"Yeah, well, I've changed my mind," the director said. "I—"

"I'd like to put a bullet in his mind," Bullseye said as she stood near Leeland, trying to take advantage of the scant shade provided by drones. But even in the shade, the average Troken temperature was well over fifty degrees Celsius, one hundred and twenty degrees Fahrenheit. This desert planet was the best place to shoot an advertisement for a drink like DreadMax, no doubt about that. *But they don't need to film players killing themselves in the heat; they just need to pan around and see all of us baking in the sun and the piles of spent* DM *bottles at our feet.*

It seemed as if the director finally got the hint that he was taking too much time with this scene, as human, Brokkr, Forge Father, Teraton, and Asterian players who were part of the shoot began to huddle around him with angry expressions on their faces. Leeland could see the little man's throat move as he swallowed, cleared his throat, and said, "Okay, one more time and then we're done. I promise. But this time, steal it from the left side."

Everyone pulled back and took their positions. All the pomp and pageantry of an actual match being played on a desert plateau would be added later graphically. But the players were real, their moves were real, and the pay was very, very real. The pay was really the only thing that kept Leeland from throttling the director personally.

Jimbo took his place near the center line. Neela stood about ten meters behind him. Guards, jacks, and other strikers fell into their places. An assistant to the director stood where the ball cannon would normally be placed. Everything was ready.

The director shouted "Action!" and the assistant tossed a bottle of DreadMax to Jimbo. He caught it and moved as directed.

Guards and jacks from the opposing team moved to try to intercept him, one required to dive at Jimbo's legs. As he had ten times before, Jimbo jumped at the right time to avoid the tackle and continued toward the back goal. He made sure he held the bottle of energy drink in his glove as if it were a real ball, ensuring that its logo and size were visible to the camera drones circling above. A jack came up and tried to steal the drink, but Jimbo left him in the dust and kept going, all the while Neela was moving closer and closer.

Through a couple more tries to bring him down, Jimbo finally reached the back goal, which was nothing more than a space in the sand marked with white paint. It too would be overlayed later with graphics and special effects.

But as required, Jimbo raised his glove to take the shot, pausing a moment to play to the invisible crowd, and then tried to throw the bottle.

Neela then appeared in the frame, pushing Jimbo a few centimeters to the right, reaching for the bottle, and plucking it right out of his glove, which he accidentally-on-purpose opened slightly to give her a better grasp. The Kalyshi striker took the bottle in her own glove, but instead of turning to score on an opposite goal, she popped open the top and downed the liquid right there, much to the shock and amazement of Jimbo.

"And... cut!"

Everyone, even the drones, seemed relieved. The director had not called a halt to this take. The scene was done, praise be! Now... a few minutes break and on to the final scene where members of both teams would huddle together on the sidelines, each enjoying a nice cold bottle of DreadMax as if the drink were so powerful and filled with so many needed nutrients and electrolytes, that it alone could bring bitter rivals together. Leeland had to keep from laughing at the thought of it, though again, he did like it, much to his surprise, and made a mental note to get Aryan to order several cases for the boys.

"Okay, everyone," the director shouted through his voice augmenter, "you have fifteen minutes to break, cool off a little, and then we'll—"

A large cracking sound, like bone shattering, echoed across the fake pitch, and the director's chest burst open.

Neela, who was standing close to the director, fell as well, screaming and clutching her leg.

Everyone else dropped or fell back, confused, looking left and right, trying to figure out what was happening, where the sound had come from.

It was a rifle report, Leeland knew. No doubt about it. He had never been in GCPS armed service, but he had spent enough time around Bullseye to know exactly what the sound was and why the director and Neela had dropped: someone was firing a sniper rifle.

For her part, Bullseye didn't duck or pause. Instead, she moved quickly to one of the SportsBlast guards and snatched his rifle out of his hands. He tried to object. "Stand down, you Zwerm!"

Leeland scrambled for cover with everyone else as Bullseye trained the guard's rifle on the ridgeline from where the shot most likely originated. The rifle had no scope. He could see that that annoyed her as she held the rifle steady on one spot, then another, and another. Finally, she pulled the trigger. It was a semi-automatic. It gave a burst of three rounds. She fired again, this time at a different location on the ridgeline, then another, and another, until the rifle's magazine was spent.

"You get him?" Leeland asked, as if even Bullseye could have found the sniper from so far away.

She shrugged. "Can't say. The shot certainly came from those rocks." She pointed to a patch of sharp granite nestled among a bed of smooth sandstone boulders and sand drifts. "I shot at all the likely places. We may never find out."

No further shots were fired from the ridgeline, and things settled.

Leeland and Bullseye moved to Jimbo. "Are you all right?" Leeland asked.

A small cadre of medibots had been brought along in case anyone suffered heat stroke. They had checked Jimbo for collateral damage. Nothing. "I'm fine, Boss," he said as he knelt beside Neela to give her comfort. She had a hole through her calf, and by the expression on her face, it was quite painful.

The director lay face down, having taken the shot straight through his chest. The medibots confirmed that he was dead.

Leeland and Bullseye turned their attention again to the ridgeline. "Who fired that shot, Bullseye?"

She shook her head. "I don't know. But we need to find out. And we need to find out who he was targeting."

"It wasn't the director, you don't think?"

"No," Bullseye said, working her jaw muscles. "Not a chance."

Chapter 19

Viper Arena and Training Complex

The sniper was found two miles from the ridgeline, cuddled up against a boulder for shade. A Veer-myn, ragged and frail, a spent Enforcer sniper rifle at his feet. It appeared as if the creature had bled out from two wounds, one in the throat, one in the back. On closer inspection of the body, however, GCPS officials found a tin of poison capsules, three missing. The green-and-red foam in the corners of the creature's mouth confirmed that it had taken its own life rather than be caught alive.

Despite an on-going GCPS criminal investigation, Leeland considered the matter closed. The assassin had been found dead, and Neela would recover in time. The director of the advert was gone, unfortunately, but otherwise, life had to move on. The Vipers' game against the Blackwing Cicadas loomed large on the horizon. Time to refocus attention elsewhere.

Bullseye walked into his office, holding a digital storage drive, an angry expression on her face. Leeland set his tablet down and tried smiling. "What's up, Boss?" He thought the question was funny. Bullseye did not.

"Turn on the overhead," she said, grabbing his tablet and pushing the storage drive into the side port.

Leeland groaned but did as she asked. A blank, green image hovered in mid-air near the desk. Bullseye tapped a few buttons, and a vid clip from her storage drive appeared.

"I've been analyzing a vid clip that one of the drones at

the shoot captured."

"Where'd you get it?" Leeland asked. "That's crime scene evidence. GCPS wouldn't have released it just—"

"Shapshir got it for me."

Of course! Why didn't he know that immediately? The resourcefulness of that fellow was growing by the day. "Okay. And?"

"And..." Bullseye said, turning the three-dimensional image in the air with a hand wave to make it easier for both of them to see at the same time. "...I know who the foul little beast was targeting."

"Really?" Leeland was impressed. "Even the GCPS forensics team hasn't made a determination on that yet."

"Yeah, well, I'll bet your salary that none of them ever served as snipers. I have. I know what I see."

"Okay, then, what do you see?"

She let the vid play in loop. Leeland watched it over and over in a matter of seconds. Even in slow motion, the bullet was moving at such a high velocity that it was difficult to see it clearly before the vid started over again.

Before playing it a fifth time, Bullseye stopped it. "There are a number of things that can affect the trajectory and flight of a bullet, Leelee: angle of the shot, the steadiness of the barrel, the recoil of the rifle itself... even wind. As we know, the Veer-myn scab was using an Enforcer sniper rifle; forensics confirmed that. But its target was neither the director of the advert nor Neela. It was firing at Jimbo."

Leeland sat upright in his chair. He stared at the paused image. "How can you tell?"

She started it again, clicking the tablet each time to allow the vid to move forward a mere fraction, then stop. "The ridgeline was about a kilometer away and one hundred feet above the film site. Give another five feet or so for the cretin in his firing position. Barrel angled down. At that time of day, the sun was just cresting its zenith, so it was a fraction or two on the right side of the shot. Sun glare on the scope would not have been much of a factor, but I suspect it was a little, given how hot and bright it was that day.

"Also, given that the scene had just wrapped, Jimbo and Neela were very close to each other, talking, giving each other compliments for the work. The director had just moved up and was giving instructions. He hadn't paused the scene this time to request another take. A lot of people were moving on and off the pitch, obscuring the sniper's shot. I also suspect that, despite our frustration over the constant reshoots, the sniper—being a Veer-myn—had settled into a routine of re-shoot after re-shoot, figuring that it could wait until the perfect shot was available. When it saw that no better shot would reveal itself, it went ahead and squeezed the trigger."

Bullseye tapped the vid forward up to the moment when the director caught the bullet in the back. She paused it. "Notice that at that moment, Jimbo and Neela are in a kind of friendly embrace, and Jimbo turns her to the left just as the bullet hits the director."

Leeland leaned forward and squinted hard. It was difficult to see. The wind and sand dust swirled up from the hard ground. Bullseye moved the vid forward two clicks. The bullet pierced the director's back and blasted out his chest. "Now watch..."

As the bullet came out the director's back, Neela's leg moved perfectly into position to receive it. Bullseye ran the video back a click, and Leeland finally saw the truth.

Jimbo's thigh had been in the position to receive the shot a fraction of a second before Neela's leg moved into the bullet's path.

"Incredible!"

Bullseye nodded. "Doubtful Jimbo would have been killed by the shot, though given the fact that it was his thigh and not his calf like Neela, the bullet might have severed the main artery, and he might have bled out before the medibots could save him. Hard to know for sure. But there's no doubt in my mind: Jimbo was the target."

Leeland leaned back in his chair and rubbed his red face. He tapped his fingers on his forehead, trying to figure it out. "Why would the little beast hit the director if his target was Jimbo? Even at such a high velocity, the bullet was slowed down by its impact into the man's back."

Bullseye shook her head. "I can't say. Perhaps the Veer-myn was just as frustrated as we were on the man's constant retakes. Figured he'd take out two birds with one stone, as they say. Even I wanted to shoot the man."

Leeland nodded. Possible, but foolish. Then again, they were talking about a Veer-myn sniper, not a fully trained Enforcer in full battle gear. The creature had been accurate to some extent, indeed, but hadn't hit his designated target. A successful failure, perhaps.

"So," he said, turning off the overhead and standing. "The question before us now is—"

"Who wants to kill Jimbo?" Bullseye finished.

Planet Gaylor

Cegrich Wick showed his back to Manan as he placed his hand on the handle of his whip. Coiled at his waist, its bloody end ran the length of his leg and hovered a centimeter from the broken tiles of the floor. The mere presence of the human annoyed him. Manan's voice made his skin crawl.

"Your patsy failed, Cegrich," Manan said, biting anger in his voice. "He hit the wrong targets."

"The Sphere is better off without that director," Cegrich said, "and who cries for an Asterian Kalyshi upstart? My thrall did his duty."

"He missed Jimbo!"

Cegrich turned, his clawed hand resting on the whip handle. He pulled a smile. "There is still time for another try."

Manan shook his head. "If you don't think that the GCPS won't figure out that Jimbo was the target, you're more ignorant than I thought. They'll figure it out, and when they do, they'll post security around him thicker and stronger than steel."

Cegrich could hear Manan shuffle towards him. The man halted a few feet away, and said, "And then, they'll find you."

Cegrich scoffed. "You overestimate GCPS abilities, my friend. I'm untouchable. A lone Veer-myn in the desert, who killed himself rather than be taken alive? The trail began and ended with him."

"He used an Enforcer sniper rifle."

"Which he could have stolen off a dead Enforcer."

"How did he get to Troken? Hmm? The planet is not known for Veer-myn infestations."

"Assassins have all manner of ways to reach their targets."

"But how does a lowly Veer-myn with questionable shooting skills make it all the way to a desert planet? And how does he know that his target will be there? Such a creature cannot know these things on his own. He had contacts, connections. And they will all lead back to you in time. You overestimate your invulnerability, my *friend*."

Cegrich growled and threw up his hands. "Fine. Be gone with you, then, if you are dissatisfied with my services."

Manan nodded. "You've failed, Cegrich. Termination of our agreement goes without saying. Nor shall you receive final payment. And wait until Mr. Carooda hears of this. Your invulnerability will be all but gone."

The one-eyed Veer-myn snarled and laid his hand back on his whip handle. "And what does he have to say about this? Why would he care?"

Manan smiled and shook his head. "We've become good friends, Le Zuan and I. Good, good friends. He vouched for your services, Cegrich, said you were the man to call for such gutter work. He put his name on the line for you. You not only failed me, but you failed his recommendation. His reach is far and wide. A GCPS investigation into your worthless assassin's movements days prior to his failed attempt... well, I'm sure Le Zuan would have something to say to them if he were so inclined." He cleared his throat. "And perhaps he will be."

"Don't push me, Manan," Cerich said, white foam now forming in the corners of his long, tooth-filled maw. "You are in my home, under my protection. Take care with your words."

"As I've said before, I am protected by powerful friends. They know where I am, whom I'm speaking to, and what I'm speaking about. Make your move, Mr. Whip, and see what happens."

At that, Cegrich backed off, slowed his breathing. He continued to snarl, raised his thin, black lips to reveal his teeth. The dark, hollow eye socket in his face throbbed. He tried squeezing the pain away; it persisted. He ignored it, like he had a thousand times before, and said, "Then be gone! Go! We shall never speak again."

He turned away, his hand shaking on his whip. Then he heard Manan behind him, chuckling. "Goodbye, Cegrich Wick. And good luck trying to eliminate Bullseye Bock."

Cegrich turned back to stare at Manan's smug face. "Yes… I know who you wish to kill. Good luck with that. And you better strike first and fast, lest she finishes the job and puts a final round into your skull."

Manan continued to chuckle as he turned toward the door to leave.

Cegrich, unable to control his anger, unfurled his whip and struck out against Manan's back, striking him between the shoulder blades. The impact of the strike hurled the human forward. He screamed in pain, lost his footing.

Cegrich pulled the whip back and struck again, and again, as Manan tried to shout for help, tried to rise and reach for the door. Large, gaping, bloody cuts formed all over Manan's back, legs, arms, as the whip's metal tip cut deep gashes through his clothing. His cries for help echoed through the room, unanswered. Cegrich paid them no mind and continued his work.

Manan shouted his last and dropped still, but Cegrich continued to strike and strike and strike until all his rage was spent.

Then he stopped. Before him, face down, Manan's lifeless body no longer chuckled, his face no longer smiled those pitiful white, clean, and straight human teeth. Manan was dead.

One of Cegrich's minions opened the door humbly and stepped in. It walked to Manan's body and stared at the mangle of bloody cuts across his back. It bowed to his master. "What—what shall we do with the body?"

"Divide it into as many pieces as you can. Burn his clothes and distribute the remains as far and as wide as possible. I wish to know his face and name no more."

Cegrich wound his whip up and attached it to his belt again. "And let's continue our work. Our target now is clear, and we must move on her soon, very soon."

"Where? And when?"

Cegrich considered. He tapped a claw on his chin. "Soon. Where... I must think on it."

Another two Veer-myn came in and helped drag Manan's body away, and Cegrich felt a chill of fear run down his prominent spine.

Was Manan telling the truth? Cegrich wondered. Had he told someone important, like Carooda, where he was and who he was talking to? If he was bluffing, then no worries. If not, then what Cegrich had just done might have been a very, *very* bad mistake. Then again, even if it were true, it would take time to gather forces against him, and that was time he could spend planning his strike against the *great* Bullseye.

The assassination attempt against Threpe had failed in one sense, but in another, it had succeeded admirably. Now, all security attention on the Vipers would be focused on protecting their star striker. No one would be protecting Carla Bock.

But where? Where do I strike? Two games left before the midseason break, then...

An idea formed in Cegrich's mind. His reservations about eliminating Manan faded as his plans for Bullseye grew.

Chapter 20

The Net, Blackwing Cicada Stadium

A Z'zor jack shattered into a dozen pieces. Tiny bits of its segmented, bug-like carapace flew everywhere as its core structure took the brunt of Shadrack's brutal slam. The guard, now back in action after his injuries, was earning his pay and then some. Unfortunately, he seemed to be the only one on the Vipers who had come to play.

"Nice slam, Shadrack, nice slam!" Bullseye shouted at Leeland's side. At least she had something to be happy about. Her guards were doing well.

"We're losing," Leeland said, feeling the urge to yell at Little Frankie to get his butt moving. The striker had been cleared to play, but he was taking it so easy it didn't seem as if he were moving at all.

"We've still got time," Bullseye said, waving rookie Cyrus in as Dillon Koch, their last veteran guard still on the pitch, took a wicked slam in the midsection and stopped moving. Two medibots flew onto the pitch and pulled him to a Sin Bin bursting with Vipers injured.

"Yeah," Leeland said, "but only if Frankie gets moving."

The only reason the Vipers were still in it was due to Shadrack and the game plan: focus on Cicada jacks and leave the rest alone. A Z'zor team was comprised primarily of jacks, faster and more agile than most other jacks in the league. Hit them at their strength, Leeland ordered, and force them to use their strikers who were less skilled than other strikers in the league. The Z'zor were a team of oddities, indeed, but no pushovers in any way.

Time was running out, and there were no more Vipers to feed onto the pitch. Everyone else was convalescing in the Sin Bin.

Frankie scooped up the ball from the striker Shadrack had pulverized and moved toward the Cicada back goal. With only one guard, the Cicadas were not using a castle, thus if Frankie could weave his way to the back goal, the Vipers had a shot to win or, at least, send the game into overtime.

The striker's left knee was bandaged, wrapped, and still a little shaky under the uniform. But this time, perhaps sensing his coach's dissatisfaction for poor game performance, Frankie ignored the knee. He twisted and turned like he had done when first recruited, pushing his full weight through that knee and leaving Z'zor strikers and jacks in the lurch while Shadrack and Me-Shan Lo tried to clear his path. Me-Shan was functioning more as a jack this game, trying to meet the Z'zor jack threat as Shadrack was doing. He was in position to score if Frankie would just throw him the ball, but no. Frankie advanced to the back goal with the ball, holding it against his body to keep sharp Cicada mandibles from plucking it away.

Shadrack slammed another Z'zor jack into oblivion as it tried to block the back goal. The creature's left arm and a portion of its left shoulder carapace broke away, bursting up into the flashing green-and-white lights of the Net. The rich, deep hiss and clapping sound of Z'zor fans ran chills down Leeland's spine. It felt like lying in bed as thousands of cockroaches swarmed over your body. Very few Vipers fans had travelled to the Net for the game. Those that had braved the trip couldn't be heard over the clicking and hissing morass that served as the Blackwing battle cry.

Little Frankie stepped into the four-point spot, moved to throw, then hesitated as another Z'zor jack tried to restrain him. The Eye in the Sky spotted the foul and called it just as

Me-Shan Lo took the jack for a ride across the pitch. Frankie moved to throw again. His hesitation this time was all in his head, Leeland knew, as no Z'zor was within four meters of the striker.

"Throw it!" Leeland shouted through the wall of angry hissing and clapping. "Score!"

Frankie's electromagnetic scoop shot out from his glove. The ball rolled along its length and flew hard and straight toward the goal.

The ball hit the goal, bounced twice, flirted with dropping in, then popped away.

Time was called, the game ended, and the Vipers lost by four.

Carooda Mansion, First Sphere, Mu'Shen'Wan Temple

Le Zuan rode the hover plank down to the floor and let it settle before stepping off. The morning's practice of the forms of the Mu'Shen'Wan had been most soothing. Being a 'gangster,' as a human might say, was stressful work. An hour in deep contemplation could settle the nerves, put the mind back in order, bring balance and comfort to the body.

He raised a teacup to his lips, drank, and ignored the first knock at his door.

"Enter," he said to the second knock as the balance began to fade.

One of his subjects stepped in and shut the door quickly. The Judwan servant bowed humbly. "It is confirmed. Manan is missing."

"Did he report his whereabouts beforehand?"

"Yes, Master Carooda," the servant said. "He went to Gaylor to speak with The Whip."

"And he has not been heard from since?"

The servant's expression turned sour. "No, Master Carooda. He did not check in afterward."

Le Zuan shrugged. "He may just be unable to make the connection."

"No, Master Carooda. There are no transmission delays."

"He may have just forgotten."

"No, Master Carooda. That is inconsistent with his behavior since first contact."

"He may just be stuck in traffic."

A joke, of course, though it was not uncommon for a slide ship to be delayed departure for whatever reason. Le Zuan waited for a chuckle from his servant, but even he knew the silliness of it.

"So, he has not been seen or heard from since Gaylor."

"No, Master Carooda."

Le Zuan sighed and shook his head. "Then it can mean only one thing."

He didn't need to say it aloud. When dealing with that Zwerm Veer-myn known as The Whip, there was only one option when things got complex, stressful: unfurl the whip and make something bleed.

Manan would never be seen again, and what did that mean for Le Zuan?

"Thank you for your report," he said, bowing. "You may go now."

The servant left quickly, leaving Le Zuan swimming in stressful thoughts.

What a stupid, stupid creature you are, Cegrich. You killed Manan too soon.

Yes, in time, the human's removal might have been necessary. But not now, and not in such a quiet manner, with no trace of his existence, no remains, no closure. Now, Kapoor

Industries would begin snooping about, and what were the odds that the trail would ultimately lead to Le Zuan? The odds were very, very good.

"Oh, Cegrich, you stupid, stupid, puppy!"

It was time to pay a visit to The Whip. A quick, brutal visit. But not immediately. It would take time for a Third Sphere corporation to muster its resources to search for their missing family member. There was time for Cegrich to try for Carla 'Bullseye' Bock, if that was indeed his target. And if he got her, all the better, for any pain brought to Leeland Roth was pain well-deserved. And if he failed, well, the GCPS would do the dirty work for him, and perhaps Le Zuan would help them in their endeavor if things got ugly.

Yes, yes, that's how it will be.

Le Zuan took a deep sip of hot tea and returned to the hover plank for more contemplation.

Chapter 21

Viper Arena and Training Complex, Press Conference

"Coach Roth! Your loss against the Blackwing Cicadas makes it all but necessary for you to win your last game against the Sons of the Green Star to even have a shot at making the midseason Ultimate match. After so many of your players were sent to the Sin Bin against the Z'zor, can you hope to win that last game?"

Leeland nodded. "Absolutely. Lots of injuries in that game, no doubt, but most are healed now. The only two players with questionable statuses are Cyrus Voh and Dillon Koch. Their situations are day-to-day."

"That's potentially two guards down going into a game against a team with the most violent Hulk guard in the FSIDL."

"The only Hulk guard, in fact," Leeland corrected. "Our other guards can handle him."

"Titus the Mighty is on pace to have fifteen confirmed kills by season end. How do you hope to stop him?"

It was a valid question, and one that deserved an answer. Leeland hated valid questions from the press; they were much more difficult to deflect. He shrugged. "It's all a matter of context and situation. Every game is different. Sometimes a player is up, sometimes down. All of the Sons' strength lies in Titus. If he falls, the rest of the team can be handled per standard DreadBall tactics."

"If *he falls."*

Leeland ignored that last comment and waited for another question.

"Coach Roth. How are you coping with all of the controversy around your brother's alleged activities with Rebs… and, of course, the allegations surrounding your potential involvement?"

Leeland sighed. "As I said at the last press conference, my focus is my team. My job is to serve the Vitala Vipers as best as I can for as long as I'm able. And I'll state again: neither I nor my brother Victor have been involved in Reb activity in the past, nor will I engage in such in the future. I support the GCPS. We are both innocent of these charges."

A reporter raised her hand. *"I've just received breaking news, Coach Roth, that Digby has suspended its investigation into your and Victor's alleged involvement with Rebel activity. How do you respond to that*?"

Leeland smiled, said, "Well, speak of the devil. Seems as if Digby agrees with me after all."

"The GCPS independent investigation will still move forward, however."

Leeland shrugged. "And we'll let them." He looked at Bullseye and Conner who were sitting beside him. "Our job is to coach the Vipers to victories, and that's what we're focused on."

The Digby news was good, however, and Leeland was most pleased. Finally, cracks were forming in these ridiculous accusations. If Digby was suspending its investigation, then the GCPS would certainly follow suit in short order. Wouldn't it?

"One more question."

Leeland pointed to a reporter in the back of the room. *"Coach Roth,"* the reporter said, *"how does it feel being an uncle?"*

Many in the room laughed. Leeland chuckled and smiled. "It's fine. Victoria is a wonderful young lady, as is her mother. We're honored to have them here at the complex. We just hope that, one day, all of this business with Vicky's father, my brother, will be laid to rest, and she can get some closure. They deserve that. Thank you all for coming."

Leeland ignored other questions hurled his way as he and his staff left the room. "Well," Bullseye said, "that wasn't so bad. And great news from Digby."

Leeland nodded. "Yeah... great news."

Bullseye tugged at his sleeve. "You don't seem happy about it."

"No, I'm thrilled," Leeland said, biting his lips. "It's just... I'm worried about Titus. It's true: he's a right son of a Zee. He could single-handedly wipe out our team."

Bullseye rubbed her chin. She nodded. "Perhaps we need some MVP help."

"Conner," Leeland said, in full agreement, "who's available?"

Conner tapped his tablet and studied the screen. "Let's see... The Enforcer and Rico Van Dien."

"Very good." Leeland's mood improved immediately. "Call them both. See which one will suit up for us in ten days."

Green Stadium

Rico Van Dien signed the contract just two days before the game. Leeland was pleased; Jimbo was livid.

"You can't honestly allow Van Dien to suit up, Boss."

"Why not?" Leeland asked.

"Cause he's a little prima donna."

Leeland chuckled. "Oh, and you're not?"

Jimbo seemed hurt by that charge. "Hey, Leeland, come on, give me a break. I've grown a lot."

"You have," Leeland admitted. "More so than I would have expected. But you know as well as I do that Frankie isn't playing his best game right now. Spencer is a true asset, but Kirkus is spotty at best, and Rollin is... well, Rollin. Another power scorer like you in our lineup gives us a strong advantage."

"What we need are guards to handle Titus."

"I know that," Leeland said, frustration growing in his voice, "but the Enforcer wouldn't sign, so we take what we can. High-powered scoring can get us the win early. That's good for all concerned."

Jimbo wanted to say more. Instead, he nodded grudgingly, clicked his helmet into place, and took to the pitch.

The Vipers and the Sons of the Green Star faced off across the center line. Leeland twitched his nose. Hobgoblins had a reputation for being the foulest-smelling creatures in the game, and the stench Leeland was experiencing right now was cloying. He considered putting on the face mask that Bullseye had provided. She had hers in place, as did Conner. They would both be with him on the sidelines today. So would Vicky, who had her mask on and was sitting quietly on the bench, next to Frankie, giggling and having good times. All was in place.

The Hobgoblin crowd roared, and that made the air even fouler. The ball was fired down the center line, and the game began.

Viper Arena and Training Complex

Aryan watched the game from his office. He had begged off travelling with the team to Green Stadium, as there was so much work to do, contracts to sign, invoices to pay. Plus, he was waiting for word from his contact in Kapoor Industries, one of the few board members who was not beholden to Saanvi. He'd know if Manan was indeed Saanvi's source for all the terrible rumors surrounding Leeland and his brother. Digby had wisely abandoned its fruitless investigation. Surely, the GCPS would follow suit. Then what? If Manan was in the field and working for Saanvi, something else would come up, and perhaps even more sinister than baseless rumors. It was important to discover the truth now, for Leeland and for the Vipers organization.

"Ooh!" Aryan cringed and leaned away from the large vid screen as Me-Shan Lo took a massive shot to the head from Hulk guard Titus the Mighty, spinning the human jack around and around. Me-Shan struck the pitch in a big life-threatening *thump!* Luckily, however, he moved once his body came to a halt. He wasn't unconscious, and he wasn't dead.

Aryan had to keep from falling into the old family habit of seeing human beings strictly as financial commodities. Me-Shan Lo wasn't just an investment; he was a person, and right now, in a lot of pain. It had taken a long while for Aryan to change this behavior on that score. Sure, he'd never been as cold-hearted and pragmatic as his sister, but Damon Kapoor's blood coursed through his veins like Saanvi's, and how many times in his youth had he heard his father frame a crisis as 'How many credits will we lose because of this?' or 'How many can we gain?' In his father's mind, the universe was nothing more than a latticework of wealth to be found and 'acquired.'

MVP Rico Van Dien leaped over Me-Shan's battered body and scooped up the ball on the bounce. Oh, what a splendid piece of work was Rico! Shorter than Jimbo, but twice as handsome. Aryan had to keep from swooning himself, as the red-and-gold armored Adonis worked his magic over the pitch. The bald, pasty-faced little hobgoblins did everything in their smelly power to stop him. But Rico dodged and leapt and slid and sprinted his way down the pitch and into a strike zone. He slid to a halt and slammed a one-pointer into the goal. It was such a magical score that even the Star fans yelped their satisfaction.

Aryan's work tablet pinged with a message. He accepted it. The calm pleasant voice of his uncle Kabir played on repeat.

"Namaste, Aryan. I hope you are well. I can confirm: Manan is indeed working with Saanvi, but he has not been seen or heard from in over ten days."

Reflexively, Aryan tried to ask a question, then remembered that his uncle's response was recorded.

It continued. *"I also poked around as requested, spoke to those... creatures that you recommended. They can confirm one other thing, Aryan. Manan was in frequent contact with a very powerful Judwan in the First Sphere. They could not give me this creature's name—they seemed afraid to utter it aloud—but said that with a little further investigation, you'd be able to figure it out in time."*

Aryan shook his head. The First Sphere was legion. How in the vast galaxy could he find one so-called *powerful* Judwan in a vast GCPS soup? A powerful Judwan? Wasn't that a contradiction? Was there such a creature?

"That is all I have for you. I hope it's enough. Vidai, Aryan. I wish you well."

The message repeated. Aryan killed then deleted it, ensuring that it was wiped permanently from his tablet's memory.

Manan had been missing for ten days, and a 'powerful' Judwan was involved. Aryan sighed and stewed on that troubling information as he watched the game.

Rico Van Dien had the ball again, and Jimbo was screaming at the MVP to toss it to him in the hobgoblins' back strike zone. But three Green Star jacks piled on Rico's back, goading each other on like children. The MVP couldn't handle the punishment nor the weight. As he fell, he tossed the ball instead to Spencer Mills who was just a few meters away. Spencer took the ball and slammed it home.

The Vipers went up by three.

Aryan turned off the vid screen and stepped out of his office. Only he and security were in the building at this hour. It was dark, save for emergency lighting along the walls, which cast just enough light to allow someone to walk around freely without bumping into anything. It was peaceful, pleasant. He closed his eyes and breathed in the silence.

What to do...

He remembered playing with his cousin Manan as a child. Their relationship had never been strong. Manan was a bully, or at least tried to be. Aryan just did his best to stay out of the way, keep his head down, and remember that his branch of the family tree was the superior one. Back then, Damon Kapoor was at the height of his power, wielding his might through control of the family business. Even at such a young age, he and Saanvi basked in their father's power and import. At those times when Manan became too much to handle, a whimpering cry and a pouty lip got the little cretin out of their playground and a good whipping.

Still, Manan was family, and there were those who cared for him. It would be nice to know what had happened. Did he grow tired of Saanvi's scheming and double-dealing and just walk away? Or, was he dead? The latter seemed more likely.

So, finding out what had happened to Manan was a priority. And what of this Judwan?

The two could be connected, though Aryan had never heard of any Judwan who would kill in such a manner; never heard of a Judwan who had killed anything, in fact. He knew of the tumultuous relationship between the GCPS and the Judwan, but how could that have anything to do with Manan and the Vipers? Perhaps the attempt on Jimbo's life had something to do with all of this. He supposed a Judwan could act as a kind of crime boss and send out minions to do his gutter work.

His mind awash with uncertainties, Aryan returned to his office, turned the vid screen on, and plopped down into his chair. Watching a little more DreadBall might soothe his nerves.

The game was drawing close to the end, the Vipers were up by one, and Titus the Mighty had Little Frankie by the throat.

***

The seven-foot, all-muscle Hulk guard tossed Frankie aside like a mangled chicken bone. The Eye in the Sky and the on-pitch referee moved closer to ensure that the slam was legal, but neither said a word as Leeland tore off his mask and shouted his dissatisfaction. "Foul! Call a foul, you idiots!"

"I don't think it's a good idea to call the refs idiots, Uncle," Vicky said, standing next to him and smiling. "They might get mad."

"I don't give a—" Leeland started to say, then checked himself. "Yeah, well, they made the wrong call. It's clearly a foul."

Vicky said nothing to that, though Leeland could tell that, despite her defense of the mechanical, non-feeling referees, she was very concerned about Frankie. So was Bullseye. So was Conner, who stood nearby, pushing Lucas Buck onto the pitch as a replacement for Frankie. He turned to Leeland. "I'm beginning to think Frankie is right, Boss. He's accident prone."

Leeland added nothing to that, other than a curt nod and a call to arms. "Tighten up, boys. Tighten up! Defend the goals."

The Green Stars had had trouble scoring all game. Too complacent, relying on Titus to shatter the Vipers so as to make scoring a proverbial walk in the park. They were looking for easy lanes of approach to Viper goals. Leeland had refused to comply.

His plan was simple: ignore Titus the Mighty altogether and play against their jacks and strikers. Whenever the brutish Hulk guard tried brushing aside a line of Vipers players, those players would scatter into multiple directions, bringing much confusion to the hobgoblin game plan and making Titus himself roar in frustration. That, too, was a tactic: make the big guy angry, and let that anger turn into mistakes.

So far, so good, save for Little Frankie foolishly trying to head-fake the big lug and getting a glove of pain right in the throat. Frankie was out, time was running down, and a Green Star striker had the ball.

Hobgoblins were notoriously bad passers, but in groups, they drew strength from each other's encouragement and could, if conditions allowed, make good plays. Leeland had not set up a castle on the back goal. He was not about to give Titus a nice, still target on which to pummel. Thus, it lay wide open.

The Green Star striker moved quickly, showing impressive speed. His name was Stinky Bink, and he'd been only one of two hobgoblins to actually score for the Green Stars. He was impressive, but on this final rush, he played the fool.

Leeland had to stop himself from shouting, "Just take a one-pointer, you fool. Score to tie!" The move was just so obvious to him and to everyone in the stadium. The Green Star fans were shouting at their striker to take the safe shot and put the game into overtime. But Stinky Bink either didn't hear their calls or refused them. His mind was set on the back goal. Courageous, perhaps, but foolish.

Titus the Mighty moved to clear a path, but Shadrack and Lucas were nipping at his heels, keeping him occupied, forcing him to turn and address them. Shadrack caught a left hook and went down. Medibots moved to collect him as two hobgoblin jacks joined Stinky Bink on his sprint to the back goal.

Jack Jerold Minata and striker Spencer Mills were waiting, neither one certain exactly how Stinky Bink would move. To the right? The left? It was hard to know. He wiggled and juked and shuffled so much that it seemed he might wear himself out before reaching the strike zone. Finally, Jerold put both boots down and waited. Spencer followed his lead, and together, they blocked the back goal from an easy score.

The Green Star striker suddenly seemed unsure of himself, as if he now realized that he'd made a terrible mistake. But no going back. No time, and there was no way any Viper would allow him to readily pick another strike zone. Now or never.

There was a gap between Jerold and Spencer. Small, but Stinky Bink was small. He aligned himself with that gap, found good footing, and took the shot.

In that split second, Jimbo stepped between the toss and the goal. He stretched his electromagnetic scoop out for a catch, only to be bumped aside by Rico Van Dien. The tossed ball flew right into Rico's glove. Time was called, and the Vipers won it by one.

Everyone on the Vipers sideline cheered. Everyone was happy. Everyone except Jimbo, who leapt into Rico Van Dien like a guard and began to whale upon his head.

Chapter 22

On one level, Leeland was quite impressed with Jimbo's fighting skills. *Maybe I'll make him a jack*, he thought, as he and Conner and half the team worked to pull the two strikers apart. On another level, he was livid.

Rico gave as good as he got, striking Jimbo in the head and chest with very precise fists. Luckily, they were both so well-armored that their pummeling did little or nothing to harm each other (although, what damage they were causing to their ball gloves remained to be seen). It gave the Hobgoblin team and fans something to laugh about, however.

Shadrack and Dillon finally managed to pull them apart. Both were hauled into the visitor locker room and dropped to the floor.

Rico pulled off his helmet and threw it down. "Forget it! I'm out of here!" He stormed out. Jimbo stayed on the floor, working to get his helmet off.

"Nice move, Jimbo," Leeland said after Rico was gone. "Your mother teach you those kinds of manners?"

"Back off, Coach!" Jimbo spat, throwing his own helmet aside and accepting Little Frankie's help to stand. "He stole my play."

Leeland nodded. "Yes, he did." He stepped closer. "It was a jerk move. But you know what you do in a situation like that? You let it go and then maybe, later, you chew his head off. Behind closed doors!"

Leeland turned away from Jimbo and addressed the entire team. "Listen up! Somewhere down the road, we're going to need more MVPs. It's inevitable. But no one, and I mean *no one*, will agree to sign with us if they have to deal with outbursts like that. You get me? MVPs are arrogant, brash, self-absorbed. I wanted to rip Van Dien's head off as well. But we're not going to do it. We're not going to give the fans or the press any excuses to question our resolve, our maturity. We're going to suck it up, like men, and play our game.

"And before you accuse me of hypocrisy, let me speak clearly: I know the mistakes I've made in my life. Don't throw them back into my face. I live with that guilt every day. But this is a new day. We move on, we do our job, and we deal. You understand me? *Do you understand me?*"

If they didn't understand, nobody said so. Some nodded, some said "yes," some just stood there, quietly, a blank expression on their faces. It was enough for Leeland. For now.

"Go," he said, "get cleaned up, get dressed, and get to the shuttle before I get mad!"

He stalked off, followed by Conner and Bullseye, into a small room designated as the visiting coach's office. It was nothing more than a closet. The perfect size for a Hobgoblin.

If he had something to throw at that moment, he'd have done so. Instead, Leeland fell into the lone chair, leaned back, and rubbed his eyes.

"Are you going to suspend him?" Bullseye asked.

"What?" Leeland asked, realizing someone had spoken.

"Jimbo. Are you going to suspend him?"

"What? No, I'm not going to do that. Nor am I going to fine him."

"The FSIDL might," said Conner. "They have rules governing that kind of behavior."

Leeland waved him off. "Let them deal with it, then. My speech was enough." He managed to chuckle. "It better be enough, 'cause Jimbo just made all our lives more difficult going forward."

***

The Vipers' win against the Sons of the Green Star put them into the Ultimate charity match with a five to three midseason record, besting the Nemion Oceanics by one game. The other three teams participating were announced two days later.

"The Shan-Meeg Starhawks, the Bremlin Nebulas, and the Daring Curcuits," Conner said, activating the vid screen in Leeland's office and showing, side by side, video of all three teams in action.

"Asterians, Kalyshi, and Metabots," Leeland said. "Oh, my aching back!"

"Two Asterian teams, technically," Conner said, "since Kalyshi are, in effect, Asterians."

"Oh, goody!" Leeland said, rolling his eyes. "That makes it *so* much better."

"I'm less concerned about Asterians than I am Metabots," Bullseye said, watching the Daring Circuits make mincemeat out of their opponent. "Being able to switch on the fly from a jack to a striker or a guard is an advantage that, in my opinion, should have been banned by the game long ago."

Leeland nodded. "But perhaps it won't be so terrible in this upcoming Ultimate match. Each team's only allowed five players on the pitch. That, plus the FSIDL rule of only one guard on the pitch per team at any given time does reduce their transformation options somewhat."

"I'm not thrilled about that rule either," Bullseye said, shaking her head. "Takes the power right out of our hands,

Leelee."

"Yes, but this is a charity match. The FSIDL doesn't want too much blood and guts strewn across the pitch when the purpose of the match is to give to those less fortunate than us." He leaned over his desk and tapped buttons to focus in on the Bremlin Nebulas. The other three games faded into the background.

"I like the rule," Conner said. "I don't want my players getting badly injured or killed in a game that doesn't matter in the final season tally."

"Then I guess I'll just stay here on Hope," Bullseye said, finding her seat. "No reason having me in this game."

"Nonsense," Leeland said. "We're still going to have guards in play. If Shadrack goes down, Dillon will come in. If Dillon, then Maddog." Leeland smiled and winked. "Come join us. I like having you around."

***

They went to *Pippi's Carne Delights*, one of Rosaria's best restaurants for succulent meat dishes. Vicky wanted to go because they had the 'best hamburgers,' as she put it. Heather liked their charred beef tips with a side salad. Leeland kind of liked their six-ounce ribeye with a spicy Asterian red sauce. He felt a little guilty partaking in an Asterian dish, what with the Ultimate match coming up in seven days. But he stowed that silliness and went with them for a pleasant meal. And besides, Vicky had begged.

"Have you decided on what charity you are going to be playing for?" Heather asked as they walked back toward the Vipers' training complex.

A small security detail that Bullseye had insisted upon walked a few paces behind them. Leeland knew it was necessary, especially given the assassination attempt against Jimbo, but he felt uncomfortable with them so nearby. He didn't feel like speaking about much of anything walking in their shadow.

"Yeah, we're going with what Conner recommended: The Rosaria Rare Diseases Research Institute. The RRDRI, I think he called it. Any proceeds the Vipers collect from the game will go to them. Any profits above and beyond what the teams make for their charities will go to FSIDL's official charity: The Heart and Hearth Children Refugee Fund. The HHCRF." Leeland shook his head. "All the abbreviations make my head hurt. But they're all good causes.

"We live in a tumultuous universe, Heather. A lot of problems, heartache, a lot of war. It's nice to do something... *nice* for a change."

She smiled, and out of the corner of his eye, he could almost see her reach out to grab his arm to pull herself close. But she didn't.

Instead, they continued walking toward the complex, with Vicky between them, holding both of their hands. The sun had set, but the light of the buildings pressing in gave them ample room to see where they were going, to see the perpetual life and energy of the city. Rosaria was a living space that never slept.

"Coach Roth! Coach Roth!"

Leeland paused. To his right were gathered a small group of, presumably, fans, who had noticed him on their evening walk about town.

First, he hesitated. Heather nudged him with her shoulder. "Go ahead. Go talk to them. You're famous around these parts."

He wasn't so sure of that, given the continued push of some very important Rosaria citizens to change the Vipers' name and official location status, but these people seemed innocent enough.

One of two security guards moved up next to him. "Just wave and move on, sir. It's not a good idea to stop."

Leeland looked the crowd over again. He shrugged. "They seem innocent enough. You come with me. If anyone makes a move, you can take them down."

"Very well, sir," the guard said.

Leeland approached them, shook hands, and began feeling good about the evening and his decision to go out to eat and have a good time.

"What's your plans for the Ultimate match, Coach?" One of the Vipers fans asked.

"Well," Leeland said, smiling broadly, "let me tell you..."

***

Three blocks away, Le Zuan Carooda's limousine hovered a foot off the curb. Inside, he and his assistant watched as Leeland's scanned image came into clear focus on the vid screen in front of them.

Le Zuan blanched. "Ugh! Does he have to be naked?"

"My apologies, Master Carooda," the assistant said, "but the scanner beam pierces clothing to ensure the best possible reading of the actual physical body."

"And it won't be detected?"

"No, sir. It's the latest technology. The scanner sits inside the palm as organic gel. Afterward, the body will absorb it and push it out as waste. It's completely undetectable. You have my word."

Le Zuan nodded but averted his eyes from the image until it had reached Leeland Roth's chest. What mattered the most to him was Leeland's face. A capture of the face mattered the most.

"Make sure you get his face perfect," Le Zuan reiterated. "No mistakes!"

"Yes, Master Carooda."

Le Zuan watched as, pixel by pixel, Leeland's face came into view. Yes... yes, that was the face he remembered, the one that had informed his dreams and threatened his nightmares for so long after the end of his career. That was the face, and just how so alike it was to his brother Victor's. They were not twins, but the similarity was shocking. Scanning Leeland's face, then, felt like scanning them both. *Wonderful... wonderful...*

"And we're done," his assistant said with much joy, making a few final adjustments to the captured image and then saving it off for later use.

"Very good," Le Zuan said, reaching for a snifter and pouring himself a blood-red wine. "Go thank our co-conspirator for his services, and... make sure he's disappeared."

"Yes, Master Carooda."

Chapter 23

Viper Arena and Training Complex

"What is our game plan, Boss?" Little Frankie asked at the final team meeting before they'd pack up the show and head to the Ultimate charity match.

Good question, and one that Leeland hadn't given much thought, in truth. He had given a game plan (of sorts) to the fans he had spoken with after dinner a few nights past, but it was more a series of generic platitudes to keep up their humor and spirits: "We're going to whip them into paste," "We're going to pop them likes zits," "Our plan is to win!" That sort of thing. Specifics? None.

"Our plan is thus," he said to the entire team assembled in the meeting room. "We're going to play our game. It's that simple. We're going to do what we've been doing from game one: strong defense backed by solid, precise scoring."

Shadrack put up his hand. "When you were in the game, Boss, did you ever play an Ultimate match?"

Leeland nodded. "Once, if I recall correctly." He chuckled. "And we got whipped pretty badly too. I don't think Trontek scored a point in that match."

"No, you didn't," Bullseye said with a wink. "One of the best games I've ever watched."

Everyone laughed, including Leeland. "Yeah, I think the winner was a Koris team, right?"

"Yes. The Wu-Ling Wanderers."

"That's right. First and last time I ever played against them. Luckily. Anyway, getting back to the subject at hand..."

Leeland tapped buttons on the podium, and the vid screen showed games of all three of their opponents. He let it play for a while, allowing his players to watch the two teams from the Star Conference. They were somewhat familiar with how the Bremlin Nebulas played their game, but not the Shan-Meeg Starhawks or the Daring Circuits, although it was quite likely that many of them might have watched game footage in their free time. But, watching a game for entertainment and watching one for the job were two different endeavors.

"Speed, speed, speed," he said, turning down the volume but letting the games play. "That's what we're up against. And with the FSIDL limit of only one guard on the pitch per team at any given time, that makes it even worse. But that does allow us to run with more strikers as well, and I'd put our strikers up against anyone anywhere."

Leeland put up two fingers. "Two balls will be in play. Five players max per team on the pitch. That's a total of twenty players at one time, though it'll fluctuate up and down as injuries mount. The Shan-Meeg Starhawks are the favorites to win, coming into the game with a seven to one record. They're formidable, but so are the Daring Curcuits. In fact, I'm more concerned about them than an Asterian team. You know where you stand with Asterians and Kalyshi. But with Metabots? A jack can be standing in front of you one second, and suddenly it turns into a guard. Don't be surprised if they risk being fouled out to turn a jack into a guard and go over the limit just to knock you into the Sin Bin forever. They're the team to watch. And, since the game will be played in an Ultimate arena in the Radner system, it's like a home game for them."

Maddog raised his hand. "Boss, which of us guards will start?"

Leeland looked over to Bullseye.

"I haven't decided yet," she said. "I'm still watching game footage. We'll make a decision on that during our slide into the Radner system."

"An Ultimate match is chaotic," Conner said, standing up from his chair. "I've heard of stories of players passing out during play simply because they can't get a handle on where they are on the pitch and where all the bodies and balls are flying. It's a madhouse out there, but remember: this game is for charity, a chance for us to represent our corporation in giving back to the community. It won't count for or against us in the season, but it matters."

"Play hard, but play smart," Leeland said, turning off the vid screen. "I know when the klaxon sounds and the game begins it's difficult to hold back. Give as good as you get, but we don't want any unnecessary injuries in this one. That's one of the reasons the FSIDL limits guards. They want a fast-paced, high-scoring game for the kiddies, not a blood fest that makes coaches and owners angry. Any last questions?"

From the back of the striker section, Jimbo raised his hand. "Will we be employing MVPs for this one, Boss?"

Leeland suppressed a smile. He couldn't tell if his star striker was trolling him or asking a serious question. It was hard to know from the look on Jimbo's face. "No worries, Jimbo. The FSIDL doesn't allow that either for this match. No one will steal your thunder in this one."

***

Leeland was disappointed but not overly surprised. "So, you've decided not to come with us to the Radner system."

Heather nodded. They were having a small, final dinner before he and the team headed out in the morning. "I've got

Vicky enrolled in a school now. She could do her work enroute, of course, but I'd prefer she stay here and concentrate on her studies. If we go with you, all she'll want to do is be by your side. She'll have no mind for GCPS history."

Sitting at the table with them, Vicky pulled a face and stuck her tongue out at her mama and then promptly went back to finishing her meal.

Leeland laughed. "I sure hope GCPS history is easier these days to learn then it was when I was her age. Corporate history is not fun to read about."

"I want to go be with Frankie," Vicky said, letting her lip quiver a little as if she were about to cry. But Leeland knew it was just for show. He couldn't help but smile. She and Frankie might be good friends, but she had learned her theatrics from Jimbo. "I want to watch DreadBall."

"You see what your players have done?" Heather said, motioning to her daughter. "Teaching her all kinds of bad manners and habits. Finish your supper, young lady, and then off you go to bed."

"Don't be too hard on them, Heather," Leeland said, wiping his mouth and pushing away from the table. "They're rough men in a rough profession. Just be glad they aren't teaching her any bad words."

"Oh no? Hang around longer, and you'll hear them." Heather helped Vicky from her chair, gave her a tight hug, and kissed her cheek. "Now, say good night to Uncle Leeland and then get ready for bed."

Leeland crouched to accept Vicky's hug and peck on the cheek. "Bye-bye, Leeland. Go kick some Zwermy butt!"

"You see? Foul mouthed!"

He patted her on the head and sent her on her way.

Leeland stood up and looked around. They were alone now, and he smiled as he turned to Heather. "I've just heard word: the GCPS is dropping its investigation of me and Victor for any Reb involvement. As far as they are concerned, we're clean."

Heather smiled. "Hey, that's good news."

But she didn't seem all that excited. "What's wrong?" he asked.

She shook her head, "No, nothing. It's just that... I never had any doubt that both of you were innocent of those charges. But... I've been thinking about my long-term plans." She sighed, rubbed her face, then said, "At some point, the season will end, and Vicky and I will have to leave."

Leeland shook his head and shrugged his shoulders. "Why would you have to leave? The Vipers are planning to be around for a long time. I've signed a three-year contract. You're welcome to stay here."

"But I need to find work."

"Plenty of job opportunities here," he said. "You like to cook. Work in the Viper complex kitchen. Don't want to do that, then work for us in some other capacity. Be an assistant to Carla. To Conner. There's no reason why you have to—"

"I don't want the DreadBall life," she said, her voice rising higher than expected. She shot a glance to the bathroom where Vicky was conducting her ablutions behind a closed door. Heather lowered her voice again. "I don't want it for me. I don't want it for Vicky."

Leeland stood there in silence, not knowing what to say. On one level, he understood her completely. Memories of Victor, what happened to him, how the game and the environment of DreadBall had shaped the kind of man he was. Not a Reb sympathizer, certainly, but no saint either. Leeland imagined that she saw her daughter growing up and falling in love with a DreadBall player that might do the very same thing his brother had done to her, or, worse, that Vicky might decide to play the game herself and find her death at the business end of a Marauder guard's fist. All valid concerns.

But there was one thing Leeland knew that, apparently, Heather did not.

No matter how hard you try to keep Vicky away from the game, if she wants it, there's nothing you can do to keep her from it.

He didn't say it out loud. It would do no good anyway. Not now. Vicky was just a child, and Heather was her mother. To try to force the issue would be foolish and do nothing but drive a wedge between them.

Instead, he smiled. "Sure, no problem. When I get back from the Ultimate match, we'll plan something together."

Heather's eyes grew wide. Her mouth opened. "Together? I didn't mean that we had to go—"

Leeland waved her off. "No, no, no. That's not what I meant. I mean, I'll help you find something. I've got contacts outside of the DB biz, you know, as do Carla and Conner. Perhaps Aryan could help you find something to do inside Kapoor Industries. Lots of options out there. I—we—can help you look."

That seemed to satisfy her. She nodded. "Okay, that will be fine." She stepped back a pace and offered her hand. "Thank you, Leeland, for a fine dinner. And as Vicky said, go kick some Zwermy butt."

Leeland laughed and nodded. "We'll win it for her. Good night, Heather. I'll catch up with you when I return."

He left the apartment and struggled with his thoughts on the way back to his office.

Their conversation had troubled him, and he was surprised at that. Perhaps he shouldn't have expected her to say anything else. When he had invited them to the complex to live, his reasons had been mercenary: to get the press off his and his family's back. There was no expectation in his mind that this arrangement would last forever. But now... Now, he had grown accustomed to their faces, as an ancient, nearly forgotten song had said. Life without Vicky underfoot would be unwelcome.

He shook his head, rubbed his face. No. Now was not the time to worry about such things. Now, an Ultimate match loomed large before him, and all his concentration needed to be focused there.

Funny, though, he thought, how Heather had misinterpreted his comment about them finding something together. What a silly notion.

Then again, perhaps it wasn't a silly notion at all...

Chapter 24

The FSIDL Ultimate Arena, Radner System

Hello to DreadBall fans everywhere! I'm Elmer...

And I'm Dobbs...

And we want to welcome you to the First Sphere Intergalactic DreadBall League's midseason Ultimate Charity Match. And what a game we have for you tonight, boys and girls.

That's right, Elmer. This one's going straight into the history books of the league, if I'm any judge of history.

I've never known you to be, Dobbs, but I'll take your word for it. Tonight's game will feature the top four teams of the FSIDL, one from each division, two from each conference. That makes it a four-team match, am I right, Dobbs?

Your math is impeccable, Elmer. Now, let's get down to business. From the Star Conference, we have the Daring Circuits, a Metabot team from the Radner Division; and the Shan-Meeg Starhawks, an Asterian team from the Cascadia Division. Speed and accuracy are the names of the game for these two teams in what's considered the strongest conference in the FSIDL right now.

Indeed, Dobbs. And from the Core Conference, we have the Bremlin Nebulas, a Kalyshi team from the Sol Division; and the Third Sphere Vitala Vipers, a Corporate team leading the pack in the Hope Division. I must say, despite their grit, I never imagined the first-year Vipers to be in this position at the midway point of the season, did you, Dobbs?

Not on your life, Elmer, which these days, isn't saying

much. I must hand it to Leeland and the crew, though: they know how to put on a good show, stumbling, rumbling, bumbling through adversity and crisis. And now they've eked out enough wins to be here tonight. I'm as surprised about it as you are when you wake up in the morning and there isn't a bill collector at your door.

Haha! You're a funny man, Dobbs. Remind me to speak to the warden about revoking your parole. But moving on, this is going to be a game about speed and accuracy. This will be a strikers' brawl, wouldn't you say, Dobbs?

I would indeed, Elmer. It's a real gut punch to a team like the Vipers who rely on a two-guard system to work their game plan. But they'll figure it out. If there's anything we've learned from Leeland Roth these past couple years, it's that he thrives under adversity.

You're right about that, Dobbs. So, any last-minute predictions for the kiddies watching from home? Who do you think will win this Ultimate match?

Well, Elmer, if the network paid me enough money to place a bet, I'd say...

***

Thousands. Tens of thousands. Hundreds of thousands. Leeland had never seen a crowd as large as the one now packed into the stadium. Not only did every team have its many thousands of fans, but so too did each charity. Then there were fans who just loved DreadBall, from all walks of life, from all economic levels, from all ages. The swirling kaleidoscope of lights; the big, booming screens of advertisements, entertainment, and past game footage of all four teams created a visual explosion that was difficult to process all at once. The decibel level was so high that the

FSIDL had to put noise-dampening screens around the arena to keep the sounds from potentially affecting the movement of the ball. Leeland put his hand on the backrest of a chair in the subs bench and felt the kinetic vibration of the arena through his arm.

"I don't recall it being this... vibrant when I played Ultimate," he said to Bullseye standing nearby.

She nodded. "Neither do I. But this is a new league in a different part of the universe. The FSIDL has its fans and is growing."

Indeed, it was. "Are you ready?"

Bullseye nodded. "Yep. I'll see you after the game." She leaned over and gave him a light peck on the cheek. "Kick some Zwermy butt!"

Leeland nodded and smiled as he watched her work her way through the team, giving each of them high fives and accepting a hug here and there before she left the Viper sidelines for the coach's booth. She'd be working the game from above; he and Conner from the sidelines.

"You ready, Conner?" Leeland asked.

He shrugged. "I suppose so. You?"

Leeland shook his head. "Nope. But let's go play ball anyway."

***

Remind the people how scoring works in an Ultimate match, Elmer.

With honor, Dobbs. The pitch is a hexagonal grid, since a total of six teams could play in one match. The FSIDL only fields four teams each year, so two segments of the grid will be cordoned off with repulsor fields that will deflect the ball if it tries to bounce into those areas. Players can be pushed through those shields, but they risk being called for a foul and sent off, so I suspect that players will give those unused areas a wide berth.

Each team has a strike zone that they must defend. Successful shots on goal in those strike zones are two points, with a bonus point given to a team making a goal from the furthest strike hex.

Just like in regular DreadBall.

You got it, Elmer.

In addition, when a team scores on one of their opponent's goals, the team scored on loses two or three points respectively. So, in essence, it's a four-to-six point swing.

Tell them about the central tower, Dobbs. Tell them about the central tower!

Calm down, Elmer, calm down. You'll have to forgive my friend here, ladies and gentlemen. He loves the central tower.

The tower that you see in the middle of the arena is where the balls are released. The tower also serves as a goal, so it can be scored upon if a player makes a strike attempt adjacent to it. That strike, if successful, gives the team one point. So, to recap scoring, a team can score in an opposing strike zone for two or three points and on the central tower for one point.

The central tower is also the referee in an Ultimate match, the Eye in the Sky, as they say. There is no physical ref on the field; all fouls are seen and called by the central tower.

So, there you have it. That's how DreadBall Ultimate works. Oh, and one final point: just like regular DreadBall, the team that scores seven points during the match automatically wins.

I don't anticipate that we'll see an automatic win, Dobbs. Do you?

Not with this passel of teams, Elmer. The scoring's going to be high and frenetic. I'm shaking just thinking about it.

You're shaking because the arena is hopping, Dobbs. As are all four teams as they take their positions on the field.

It's time to start, ladies and gentlemen. Grab a drink and a snack, and click your seat belt into place. It's time to launch the first ball.

Chapter 25

The first ball launched from the central tower struck a repulsor field, ricocheted back toward the tower, struck the tower, and ricocheted into the glove of a waiting Nebula striker. Players from the three other teams moved to intercept, and the game was on.

The Nebula striker was not the Kalyshi that had been wounded during the filming of the advertisement, but Leeland had seen her in game footage many times. She was good. They called her The Grip, for once she had the ball in her glove, it stayed there until she was either knocked out of the game or she scored. Not a single steal attempt had worked on her all season, but Little Frankie gave it a shot.

The Grip moved toward the central tower. Made sense to Leeland: get a quick one-point strike to set the tone. She moved like a strand of smoke, twisting and turning to deflect the reaching metal arms of a Daring Circuit jack in the middle of transforming into a striker. The transformation succeeded, the Metabot striker reached for the ball, and failed with a face-down slide into the legs of the lone Asterian guard standing there as if he were waiting for something to happen. But Little Frankie was quicker.

He moved in counterclockwise motion against the impetus of The Grip. His intention was clearly not to snatch the ball off her glove; that would be a fool's errand. Instead, he balled up his fist as if he were going to throw a punch. As The Grip moved her glove to make a strike against the central tower, Little Frankie's little fist punched through the tangle of arms and struck the ball as it took flight toward the tower.

The Grip could breathe a sigh of relief, for Little Frankie did not 'steal' the ball from her (her record was intact). Instead, it went flying out of her glove and into the surprised possession of that Metabot jack who had just transformed into a striker. The Metabot caught the ball much to its surprise, paused a moment to receive light-speed commands from its sideline programmer, then slammed the ball into a central tower goal.

The Daring Circuits fans shook the arena, and the Metabots were in the lead by one.

***

Wow, that was fast!

You are so right, Elmer. I don't think Viper striker Little Frankie meant for it to work out that way, but as they say in the Ultimate arena, 'Nothing ever works as planned in an Ultimate match.'

You've been watching too many silly color commentators, Elmer. But there is a lot more play to go.

***

Both balls were launched into the arena simultaneously. One flew toward the Starhawks' strike zone, the other toward the Vipers' strike zone. Jimbo was on that ball right away.

He scooped it into his glove and moved toward the central tower. Another Metabot was transforming into a guard as he passed it, but it appeared to have failed the test, as sparks of electricity popped along the seams of its blue-black body. Then, it shut down momentarily before rebooting and continuing as a jack. Shadrack slammed into the Metabot and crushed it against the central tower, giving Jimbo a clean shot on goal. He took it and scored.

The ball was relaunched into play. This time, it flew toward the Nebula strike zone.

Despite an ample number of vid screens on the tower itself and around the arena, Leeland found it difficult to see the entirety of the pitch. "I can't see what's happening on the other side of the tower," he shouted through the comm link to Bullseye. "What do you see?"

"Everything," she said, sitting next to Shapshir Goethe in the coach's booth. "There's a mad scramble for the second ball between the Starhawks and the Nebulas. Looks like the Asterians are getting the best of that exchange."

And just as she said that, a Nebula jack coldcocked the Asterian striker who had just received the ball on a short throw. The striker went down hard and did not move.

"Never mind," Bullseye said with a sigh and a laugh.

The ball the Asterian was holding popped off his glove and into the waiting hands of a Metabot jack, who then tried to toss it to another team member. But Jimbo flew into the path of the tossed ball and deflected it off his glove, sending the ball whirling at a cool one hundred fifty miles per hour into the Asterian guard's back. The ball strike knocked the guard off his feet, and he went flying into Little Frankie, who was moving to intercept the ball. Little Frankie stumbled into a Kalyshi jack who tried to dodge away but also fell sprawling in the comic chain of events.

The result of this domino effect was for the ball to ricochet off the central tower and right into the waiting glove of another Asterian striker, who now moved to score against the Vitala Vipers strike zone.

"Keep tight, Jerold," Leeland screamed from the Vipers sidelines. "Keep tight!"

Jerold Minata was the lone man waiting in the Vipers strike zone. He pedaled back a few paces to keep himself between the goal and the charging Asterian striker. There was no one moving to intercept the Asterian; Jerold was it.

Even through the jack's dark protective visor of his helmet, Leeland could see, almost feel, Jerold's anxiety. *Don't worry about it, buddy,* Leeland said to himself as he watched the potential train wreck coming. *Just play and have fun.*

It mattered if they won the game, of course, because if so, then the Vipers charity would get a massive amount of bonus FSIDL megacredits. But no need for any player, on any team, to get all bent out of shape about one score or another. There was still plenty of time left in the game, and with two balls in play at once, anything could happen.

Leeland kept his mouth shut and watched the play unfold.

The Asterian striker stopped his swift charge against the Viper goal. He slid into the furthest point from the goal to try a three-point shot. Jerold braced for the throw. The Asterian launched the ball, and Jerold jumped into the air to deflect it.

But wait! The Asterian striker hadn't launched the ball. Instead, as Jerold leapt for the deflection, the striker stepped to his left, leaned in at a forty-five-degree angle, and launched the ball for an *easy* two-point score.

***

And that, ladies and gentlemen, is why the Shan-Meeg Starhawks are the team to beat in the FSIDL. Tears are literally streaming down my face. That was so beautiful.

Yes, yes it was, Dobbs. Now, stop crying before you embarrass me.

You need to get in touch with your gentler side, Elmer.

I promise I'll enroll in your yoga and meditation class after this game, Dobbs. But for now, back to the matter at hand. What a score! The Starhawks are now in the lead with two points, followed by the Daring Circuits with one, the Bremlin Nebulas are at zero, and now so too the Vitala Vipers. Oh, how quickly the fortunes of DreadBall change in this madcap arena.

***

And just like that, the teams seemed to forget the central tower and moved to score on each other's goals.

A Daring Circuit jack caught the ball from the launch and moved to score on the Starhawk goal. It transformed into a striker on the approach, but the Asterian guard who had taken a nasty ball shot into his back had recovered and was now in pursuit. Oddly enough, Metabot strikers were slower than their jack base-line physiology, and Leeland could never figure out why. Then again, he wasn't a Metabot programmer, and in this moment, he didn't care. Both the Asterian guard and a Kalyshi jack slammed the poor robot into oblivion, leaving bits and pieces of it strewn over a wide swath of the arena floor.

The massive audience loved it, bringing their collective, joyous howling and screaming to such a level that even the decibel dampeners could not keep the wall of sound from reaching the pitch. Leeland did not know if the added volume affected the flight of the loose ball, but it happily dropped right into Little Frankie's glove.

Now both Frankie and Jimbo had the balls. Jimbo had snatched his on the other side of the tower while the Metabot striker was being smashed to pieces.

"Strike the same goal!" Leeland shouted, though he doubted anyone heard him, save for Bullseye who was herself screaming at the top of her lungs, begging Leeland to get Shadrack moving to assist. He did as she requested, but it was doubtful that Shadrack could hear him. The wall of sound was too great.

The Viper strikers were on their own, and they didn't move to strike the same goal. Instead, Jimbo moved toward the Starhawk goal; Little Frankie toward the Circuit goal.

As the only guard on the pitch, Shadrack hesitated. Should he defend Jimbo or Frankie? He was closer to Frankie's position by a couple steps, but Leeland could tell that the big guy was not sure. Jimbo had the better chance of scoring, but Frankie was closer to his strike attempt. He chose to defend Jimbo. Big, big mistake.

Jimbo did a few of his patented, arrogant moves, made the ladies in the crowd swoon for his greatness, and then rifled it into the goal for two points. Shadrack's move to aid the prima donna was useless, and he suffered the consequences. A Metabot jack, in violation of the rule of one guard on the pitch per team, transformed into a guard and slammed Shadrack into the central tower. The foul klaxon sounded with red and yellow lights and ordered the Metabot off the pitch, but Shadrack was done. A medibot flew down from the ceiling of the arena and snatched the limp Viper guard away before he suffered even more punishment.

Little Frankie moved on his own to try to put the ball into the Circuits' goal, but a Nebula striker snatched the ball out of his scoop and scored herself.

***

"I hate Metabots!"

Bullseye screamed it into Leeland's earpiece. From her perch on high, she could see her boss cover his head with both hands. He said, "You and me both. Now... who do you want to send in as a replacement?"

"Dillon. Get him in there, now!"

She could see Dillon Koch slam on his helmet and enter the pitch while the broken Shadrack was dropped into the Sin Bin. She breathed a sigh of relief. He was moving, thankfully, so he wasn't dead.

If this were a regular season game, she'd have subbed in the Maddog, but despite the slam on Shadrack, Dillon was faster, quicker. They needed speed right now against these very fast teams.

Her throat was desert dry and scratchy. "You got any more of those mimosas?" she asked Shapshir, who had recovered from her shouting and now sat upright in his chair. "I need a drink."

He shook his head. "No. I keep ordering more, and the order never seems to go through. I'll go check it out in person."

Bullseye nodded, keeping her eyes on the game. The Starhawks had just scored on the central tower. The game now stood at two points for both the Vipers and the Nebulas, one point for the Starhawks, and zero for the Circuits. "And get me some choco-chips if they have any."

Shapshir left the room. Now, Bullseye was alone. Security was held outside the coaches' booths to ensure that the guards themselves were not spies for the opposing teams.

The energy of the crowd shook the booth. The light spectacle made it difficult for her to see the action on the pitch, but she managed. And she liked being in the booth. It was less chaotic, less nerve-wracking than being on the sidelines, as Leeland and Conner were at the moment.

The wave of crowd noise rose again as a Metabot jack scored on the central tower and a Kalyshi jack was sent to the Sin Bin. And just like that, every team in the game had at least one point.

Bullseye winced at her scratchy throat. “Shapshir!” she said, though the Asterian assistant had not returned. “Where’s my mimosa?”

Chapter 26

I must say, Elmer, it's been a lower-scoring game than I would have imagined. But an exciting one. Wouldn't you agree?

I would indeed, Dobbs. I've been agreeing with you a lot in this game, more so than I usually do.

You've seen the light!

Or the darkness. Whatever the case, we're coming down to the close of this fast-paced smash fest. Who's going to pull it out, Dobbs?

Hard to say Elmer, but I think I'll change my previous prediction and lay all my chips on...

***

The Daring Circuits and the Bremlin Nebulas scored nearly simultaneously on the central tower, and thus, the game stood at three for the Nebulas, two for the Vipers and the Circuits, and one for the Starhawks. Despite their clear speed advantage, the Starhawks were finding it difficult to penetrate the clot of bodies in the center of the arena. Now that the game was drawing to a close, everyone was huddled around the tower, fighting for the balls in a brawl of arms, gloves, fists, and legs.

Leeland stood on tiptoes, trying to find his strikers beyond the tower. Little Frankie had voluntarily checked himself out due to a reoccurring limp from a previous injury, and so it was Jimbo and Spencer scrambling for balls. Both Jerold Minata and Lucas Buck were guarding the Vipers goal, so only Dillon Koch was left for fist work. He was doing his best.

With his left fist, he put down a Metabot jack in mid-transformation. With his right, he coldcocked the Starhawks guard. But that Asterian was as tough as nails, and so he answered the punch with one of his own, driving Dillon back into the pile of bodies currently fighting for the ball. That push back, fortunately, caused the ball to pop out of the pile and bounce down the pitch toward the Nebula goal.

Spencer was after it immediately, as were three other strikers. The ball bounced and ricocheted through the hands of the Nebula jack guarding their goal and right into the electromagnetic scoop of Spencer Mills, who considered a shot on the Nebula goal, then turned and tossed it back to Jimbo who stood alongside the tower and had a clear shot.

Jimbo took the pass and slammed it into the tower.

The arena shook, a mad array of colored lights and lasers spread through the hot air, and the Vipers now held the lead with the Nebulas.

And time was running out.

***

Bullseye leapt from her chair and clapped loudly. The game didn't matter for standing in the league, but still, a win was a win, and the bragging rights coming out of this one would be wonderful. It wouldn't hurt her chances at snagging a head coaching job next season, either.

She hadn't thought of that in a long, long time. Leeland was no dummy; he knew that she had only signed a one-year contract for that very reason. She didn't need a head coaching job; she could stay with the Vipers for as long as they would have her, and she'd be an important asset each day. But her short time as head coach for the Banshees during the Third

Sphere tournament had made her realize that she could lead her own team. It was an experience and a thrill that she had not forgotten. *If we win this game, my stock goes way, way up.*

She put the notion out of her mind and felt another aggravating scratch in her throat. She coughed. *Where is Shapshir?* She looked toward the door. No one. The game was ending. The Vipers were tied for the lead, but they hadn't won it yet. One more strike without any counterstrikes, and they'd take home the trophy, their charity would cash in, and life would go on.

A Starhawk jack snagged one of the balls. Bullseye refocused her attention to the field.

The door to the coach's booth opened.

"Finally," she said, without turning around, "I was beginning to wonder where you were. I hope you brought enough snacks and mimosas for an army, because I'm as parched as—"

The last things Bullseye Bock felt and heard was the crack of a whip, the tight squeeze of a leather cord around her neck, and the crack of a club across her face.

***

A Starhawk striker had one of the balls, time was running out, and Conner tried desperately to reach Bullseye through his earpiece. "She's not responding."

Leeland's attention was fixed on the pitch. The Asterian striker was moving to score in the Nebulas' goal. His own strikers were flailing to find the second ball in the pile near the Metabot side of the pitch. "It's probably just a bad connection," he said, waving it off. "Don't worry about Carla. Let's try to steal that ball from that Asterian striker. Move

Jerold to intercept."

Doing so would weaken their defensive stance at their own goal, but the game was ending. It hardly mattered now, even if an opponent snagged the second ball and tried to score on their goal. Allowing the Starhawk player to score a two-pointer on the Nebulas' goal could mean that the game would end with the Starhawks and the Vipers tied three to three. Leeland had no desire to play a one-on-one overtime period with the best team in the league.

Conner barked the order to Jerold, and the human jack moved to intercept. A fruitless endeavor, perhaps, but he was the best jack the Vipers had on the field right now.

The Starhawk striker, known as Jubyl Shook, was not the one that had made Jerold look foolish earlier in the game. Shook was smaller, thinner, not one of the Starhawks' best scorers, but he had the ball and was making his move.

On the other side of the tower, the bouncing ball finally found its way into the hands of a Metabot jack, who promptly slammed it home into the central tower, bringing the Circuits score up to three. Now, three teams were tied for first place. The only way the Starhawks could pull it out was to score a three-pointer.

Jubyl Shook shrugged off a grab by the Kalyshi jack who protected the Nebula goal. His little juke sent her screaming into Dillon Koch, who had broken from the scramble for the second ball to support Jerold's move to intercept. Both he and the Kalyshi jack skidded across the floor, throwing fists at each other.

Jubyl stepped into the furthest strike point from the Nebula goal. Jerold leapt into his path.

But the second ball was launched back into play, and as luck (or plan) would have it, it flew out of the launcher on the Nebula side of the pitch. At over one hundred sixty miles per hour, it struck Jerold in the side of his armor and pushed him away from the Asterian striker.

Without anyone left to harass his attempt, Jubyl Shook threw the ball into the Nebula goal from the furthest strike point, gaining three points and winning the game.

***

Oxygen! I need oxygen!

Someone get a bottle of the good stuff for Dobbs. And one for me too. I can't believe what just happened. Can you, Dobbs?

Obviously, no. For the ball to fly out of that cannon, in that direction, at just the appropriate time... well... fate must have had the Starhawks' number today.

Or a hefty bribe.

Are you suggesting corruption, Elmer?

Me? Heaven forfend! I wouldn't dream of it! But... it wouldn't surprise me if the three other teams submit official complaints to that end.

Well, we'll find out soon enough. For the time being, however, the game has ended. The Starhawks pulled out a miracle, leaving the Nebulas with no points, and the Vipers and the Circuits tied for second. Wow... what a stunning conclusion.

I tell you, Dobbs, the FSIDL gets more exciting season after season.

It does, indeed, Elmer. So now, thank you to everyone who has tuned in for this fantastic Ultimate match. I'm Dobbs, and this is Elmer... signing off with a fond, fond farewell.

***

Leeland followed the Vipers into the locker room. There was disappointment and a touch of anger on everyone's faces, but in truth, he was pleased. Only Shadrack had suffered a serious injury during the game. Everyone else had come out relatively unscathed. In another week, the season would resume, and in all honesty, it wasn't terrible to finish tied for second place. To go head-to-head with three other teams that were, in many ways, superior to the Vipers was an achievement. The Vipers' charity would not receive that massive boost of megacredits now, but they'd receive something.

"Are we going to submit a formal complaint?" Conner asked as they cleared the locker room door and waited for it to shut.

"For that last launch of the ball?" Leeland nodded. "Might as well, for I'm sure the Circuits programmers and the Nebulas coaches will do so as well. But I wouldn't expect any change in the outcome. It was a charity match. It's over."

He turned to the players. "You did good tonight, gentlemen. Good, solid play, no major mistakes. I'm proud of you."

"Thanks, Coach," was mumbled by a few, but everyone was exhausted and just ready to hit the showers and reach the slide ship to get out of the system.

Dillon stepped up "How's Shadrack, Boss?"

Leeland shook his head. "He's being looked at by our physicians. We should have an answer soon as to the extent of his injuries. Can you go check on that, Carla? Carla?"

Leeland looked around. Bullseye was not with them. He palmed his comm link. "Carla, are you there?"

Nothing. Just static.

Leeland screwed up his face. "Where the Zee is she?"

***

Bullseye opened her eyes to darkness and motion. Her head ached. She could tell that part of her face was swollen. She tried reaching up to her cheek, but her hands were tied behind her back.

She panicked. She struggled against her restraints, but her ankles were tied together as well. She moved like an eel, a worm trapped in a small space with no egress. She tried to speak, but her swollen face and mouth formed her words into meaningless moans and yelps. That, and the gag covering her mouth.

Then she smelled something foul. A combination of rotting meat, fermented juice, and bacterial growth. Smoke, too, as if someone nearby was sucking on a pipe. The smells combined to make her stomach churn.

Someone, something, was breathing close to her. Even with a bag on her head, she could feel delicate tendrils of breath curl their way through the thin fabric and tickle her nose. A foul breath, not the smells that she had detected, but something worse, something guttural and base, like an evil wind that she recognized, had smelled before.

She struggled and cried out to be released.

The bag was yanked from her head. The light of the space she was in stung her eyes, and it took several moments for them to adjust. As they did, a face came into focus in front of her. Not a human face, but one possessing a long snout with rows of sharp, uneven fangs. One lone eye darted back and forth as it studied her face. The other eye wasn't there, but a deep, dry black hole that sounded like crumpled paper when it winked.

A sharp tongue ran along the tip of the creature's fangs. "Hello, Carla 'Bullseye' Bock." The hollow eye socket crinkled and winked again. "Remember me?"

THE END

About the Author

Robert E. Waters has sold over 85 stories and nine novels, many of which have been published by Winged Hussar. He had written several stories set in Eric Flint's Alternative History series, 1632, including two Baen novels co-authored with Eric Flint (*1637: The Transylvanian Decision*), and Charles E. Gannon (*1636: Calabar's War*). Robert's story, "Ill Met in Mordheim", was published by The Black Library in 2007 (*Tales of the Old World*). His short story, "Rotten Letters", written with Jason Waters, appeared in the horror anthology, *The House on Dominion Street*. Robert has also written the Dreadball novels set in Mantic Games' Warpath universe (*The Last Hurrah*). Robert has worked in the gaming industry for 30 years as writer, designer, producer, and voice-actor. He currently lives in Baltimore, Maryland.

CB
The Last Hurrah
R.E. Waters

The Swords of El Cid
Robert E. Waters

CITY OF THE GODS - STARYBOGOW
THE CROSS OF ST. BONIFACE
ROBERT WATERS

TALES OF PANNITHOR
RISE OF THE CELESTIANS
KINGS OF WAR
C.L. WERNER